CLIMB AWAY!

A Mountaineer's Dream

▲ ▲ ▲ ▲ ▲ ▲

Deborah Parks

SILVER BURDETT PRESS

Parsippany, New Jersey

Acknowledgments

This book owes its existence to Malcolm Jensen—the editor and friend who decided I should write down my climbing stories. The design and art reflects the work and talent of Marie Fitzgerald, Susan Havice, BIG BLUE DOT, and Stephen Wells. Special thanks goes to employers who have understood my love of climbing—Lois Berlowitz, Susan Katz, Darrell Kozlowski, and Lisa Quiroz.

On a more personal level, my climbing has drawn support from a number of people. Susan Buckley taught me about the adventure of travel. Daniel Letendre showed me how to rock climb. Dan Zinkus, Fran McLoughlin, Richard Foerster, and Emily Krahn never tired of hearing about the climbs. While I traveled the world, Rich Parks kept the house intact. Kay Seeberger—a 90-year-old humanitarian—believed her prayers got me up and down the peaks safely. And most of all, I thank my Down's Syndrome sister Cathy Keeler who proved long ago that courage has no limits.

Text © 1996 Deborah Parks
Illustrations © 1996 Stephen Wells

Published by Silver Burdett Press
A Division of Simon & Schuster
299 Jefferson Road, Parsippany, NJ 07054

Designed by BIG BLUE DOT

Manufactured in the United States of America
10 9 8 7 6 5 4 3 2 1

Library of Congress Cataloging-in-Publication Data
Parks, Deborah.
Climb Away! a mountaineer's dream/by Deborah Parks;
illustrated by Stephen Wells. p. cm.
Summary: One woman's adventure on the way to
becoming a skilled mountain climber. Locales include Turkey,
Nepal, India, East Africa, and Mexico. Focuses on the training,
gear, and attitudes necessary to climb at altitude.
1. Parks, Deborah. 2. Women mountaineers—United States—
Biography. I. Title
BV199.92.P38A3 1996
796.5'22'092—dc20 95-8684 [B] CIP
ISBN 0-382-39093-8 (LSB) ISBN 0-382-39094-6 (PBK)

Who Says?

"Do you know what your gravestone is going to read?" asked my mother. "It will have just two words—*Who says?*"

When I was a child, my mother threw these words at me whenever she caught me in some daredevil stunt. Other kids in my neighborhood might like to ride bikes or play house, but I had three other games that I liked much better. I loved belly surfing down a waterfall into the local swimming hole. I also loved swaying like a pendulum in the skinny tops of trees. My favorite was scrambling up the five cliffs at Bash Bish Falls, a spectacular waterfall along New York's South Taconic Trail. Once at the top, I'd stand on the highest rock I could find and stare south to Stissing Mountain. Beyond lay the white granite cliffs known as the "Gunks," or Shawangunks (SHON-gums). At age eight, I didn't know that one day I'd climb these cliffs, too.

Each time my mother caught me in one of these stunts,

she'd warn me of the dangers. She'd yell: "You'll drown in that waterfall." "You'll crack your head when that tree limb breaks." "You'll break an arm or leg on those cliffs." To each warning, I shot back: "*Who says* I'll drown?" "*Who says* I'll crack my head?" "*Who says* I'll break an arm or leg?" Exasperated, my mother would grumble: "*Who says* you wouldn't be better off on the ground with your brother and sisters?" I'd close my eyes and sigh, "Now she's going to tell about my gravestone again." And she usually did.

More than thirty years later, I could still hear my mother's voice as our airplane nosed into Atatürk Airport just outside of Istanbul, Turkey. I had come to this ancient land to climb Mount Kackar, a 12,893-foot peak in the Pontic Mountains of eastern Turkey. Plenty of people had tried to talk me out of it. "You've never climbed a mountain," said some. "You've never been out of North America," said others. "You've never even been in a sleeping bag," said still others. Almost all of them warned: "You're going to get into trouble." I might not have had a good answer for the first three objections. But I had a tried-and-tested response for the last one: *Who says?*

As I stared in bewilderment at the crowded airport, I wondered if I might have finally said "Who says?" just one too many times. This wasn't Hollowville, New York, the farm town where I grew up. It was Istanbul, Turkey, a city that straddles the continents of Europe and Asia. Staring at the unfamiliar surroundings, I felt a knot of fear in my stomach. I compared my clothes—a baseball cap, T-shirt, blue jeans, and trekking boots—to the clothes worn by Turkish women. Most wore blouses, ankle-length skirts, and scarves. A few wore long robes and veils. None wore pants. "You're in a Muslim country," I reminded myself. "Women often keep their arms, legs, and heads covered." I began to wonder what it would be like for a woman with a baseball cap to make her way up into the Turkish mountains.

I listened for English, but heard none. I only knew two Turkish phrases: *merhaba* for "hello" and *ben Amerikan* for "I'm an American." (By now, I realized my clothes screamed out "I'm an American.") Luckily, the airport signs were in several languages, including English. Sign by sign, I made my way to the baggage claim.

Trunks and suitcases spilled onto the luggage belt. As they spun around, people grabbed them and the crowd thinned. I watched intently for my duffel bag. But it never appeared. A wave of panic spread over me. I needed my gear—sleeping bag, water bottles, dried food, headlamp, and so much more—to make it up Mount Kackar. But one thing scared me more than setting out without my gear. That was not trying Mount Kackar at all. So, with passport in hand, I headed toward customs. I thought: Well, Mom, *who says* I can't handle Turkey on my own?

After asking about my lack of baggage, the customs agent rattled off the usual questions. "How long will you be here?" "Where are you staying in Istanbul?" "Where are you going?" "Are you traveling alone?" He arched his eyebrow at my answers to the last two questions. "Not many single women head into the Turkish mountains," he explained. He then added, "Especially if they don't have

3

any baggage."

I still didn't know what I'd do about my lost gear. But I certainly didn't plan on tackling the mountains solo. Even the most experienced climbers team up with others. I planned to do the same. When I told this to the agent, he asked, "Who are these people?" I smiled and said, "I don't know. I haven't met them yet." As he shook his head, I wandered off to find a phone to call the Kariye Hotel, the starting point for the climb.

Climbing a mountain—especially one outside the United States—takes a lot of planning. A mountain-climbing group in California had set up the Mount Kackar climb. Only a few people had signed up to go. But I expected that we'd have a lot in common. There was a good chance we all liked adventure. We probably didn't mind taking risks. Because not all risks pay off, I bet most of us had tasted failure in our lives. And we probably all had a little rebel in us. I thought: there's bound to be somebody else who had asked "Who says?" as a child.

The hope of finding like-minded people had lured me into the mountains. Yet I worried about my lack of experience. Everyone had trekked, or taken extended wilderness hikes. That meant they knew how to camp and carry heavy loads. Some had done high-altitude climbing or mountaineering. That meant they knew how to deal with altitude—heights far above sea level where the oxygen grows thinner and thinner. They also knew how to scramble, or climb over boulders, and how to tie into ropes to walk across snow and ice. Two members of the team did

4

technical rock climbing. In technical rock climbing, or "free climbing," climbers head straight up rock faces. Sure they used rope and specialized equipment, but this gear is only backup in case of a fall. What free climbers rely on the most is their skill. Using just their hands and feet, they work their way up along thin edges, cracks, and whatever other "advantages" the rocks give them.

We had all written profiles of ourselves before the trip. I wondered what the rest of the team thought about having an extra inexperienced climber along on the journey—especially a climber who had lost all her gear. I'd find out soon. I dropped several Turkish coins, called lira, into the phone and dialed the hotel. A thickly accented voice said someone would come for me. "Just be patient," directed the voice. "In Turkey, things take time."

Propped up against a pillar near the airport exit, I tried to envision the Pontic Mountains. For me, mountains meant the Catskills of the mid-Hudson Valley in New York. On sunny days, my mother would point to the Catskills and ask: "Can you find Rip Van Winkle's body in the mountains? There's his head and his stomach. Can you find his feet?" When it thundered, she'd tell her four children, "Don't be frightened. That's just Rip Van Winkle's ghost bowling in the mountains."

When I asked my father if the mountains were really blue, he answered with a question. "Why don't you climb them and find out?" I'd reply, "I can't climb mountains." He'd smile and say, "Who says you can't? Have you tried?"

Maybe my father taught me to say "Who says?" He certainly supported my decision to climb waterfalls, cliffs, trees, or anything else as a child. Some neighbors said my parents were raising a "hellion," or mischief-maker. I prefer to think they raised a mountain climber.

The sound of my name interrupted all the daydreams. "Deborah! Deborah!" yelled a voice. I looked up and saw a young man in a baseball cap, T-shirt, cutoff jeans, and trekking boots. He ducked quickly under the arms of the guards at the airport exit. "I'm Jack. Let's get out of here before the guards grab me. By the way, I'm your guide up the mountains. I read in your profile that you wanted to learn how to climb. Well, let's get started."

Jack, an Oregon climber, had lived and taught in Turkey. He turned to the guards close on our heels and spun off a couple of sentences in Turkish. They made a few threatening gestures and then pointed toward the exit. Just outside the doors, a big empty bus sat at the curb. "Climb aboard," ordered Jack. I blurted out, "I lost all my gear. Can I still go on the climb?" He thought for a minute and said, "I bet it got stuck on another plane. Don't worry. We'll track it down and have a horseman bring it to you in the mountains. Otherwise, you'll share some of my gear."

As the bus headed up a twisting Istanbul street, I felt part of some fabulous fairy tale. Who knew where this magical journey would lead me? I dared to hope that it would take me to the top of Mount Kackar. What I didn't dare to hope—at least not yet—was that it would carry me to mountains all around the world.

The First Time

The bus seemed to slip deep into the past as it cut through an opening in the Theodosian walls, fortifications built more than 1,500 years ago. Our hotel lay on the other side of what is known as the Edirne Gate, in Old Istanbul. The Greeks, who built the city some 2,700 years ago called it Byzantium—a glittering trade port that hosted merchants from Africa, Europe, the Middle East, and China.

In its long history, many conquerors had claimed the city. The Persians pounced on it in 512 B.C. Celtic tribes, known as Gauls, tried to overrun it in 279 B.C. The Romans seized it in 193 B.C. and added to their empire. In A.D. 324, Emperor Constantine renamed the city Constantinople in his honor. The city survived long after Rome collapsed and the rest of Europe slipped into the Middle Ages. Christian and Muslim troops clashed over Constantinople in the Crusades. Then, in 1453, the Ottoman Turks thundered into Constantinople and renamed it Istanbul. With their arrival, Islam came to the city and the rest of Turkey.

I had studied history in college. I later taught it. And today I earn a living writing about it. Now I found myself in the heart of one of the oldest pockets of living history in the world. Next to my hotel, the rulers of great empires had built their palaces. "What do you think?" asked Jack as we arrived at the hotel. One word seemed to sum up my feelings: "Wow!"

By this time, the rest of the climbers had already gathered in a garden. Like me, they all looked glassy-eyed from jet lag. We had come from all over North America, including Canada and Mexico. Before heading up to my room, I introduced myself as the "gearless climber" from New York. "Well, you've learned your first mountaineering lesson," said one climber from Chicago. "Lug as much as you can onto the plane. Wear double sets of clothes. Stuff socks and underwear in your day pack. Above all, hang onto your sleeping bag."

People dipped into their backpacks to donate gear. Slowly a small pile sprouted on the floor of my hotel room: a wool shirt, a windbreaker, a poncho, a bandanna, moleskin for blisters, iodine tablets to purify water, and a sheet of plastic to place under a sleeping mat. Nobody had an extra backpack. But the hotel supplied a Turkish kilim —beautiful carpet for covering a floor, wall, or bed. This kilim did double-duty as a gear sack and a blanket.

As I ran my hand over the tightly woven rug, the hotel clerk said, "It comes from the mountains, you know. When the snows close the upland pastures, Yuruk herdswomen shear their goats and weave these rugs."

My makeshift pack excited me. At least with a kilim strapped to my back with a rope, nobody would accuse me of being a gear junkie—someone who likes fancy state-of-the-art gear more than climbing. I felt like the mountains had given me a special gift.

Exhausted by travel, I ate an early supper and crawled into the last clean bed I'd sleep in for more than two weeks. At sunset, the voices of Muslim prayer-callers rang out from mosques throughout Istanbul. Five times a day, Muslim men and women face Mecca, the birthplace of Islam, and kneel in prayer. "No need for an alarm clock," Jack had told me. "You'll know the time of day by the sound of Arabic prayers." As I closed my eyes, I took comfort in the muezzins, or prayer-callers, who now lulled me to sleep and who would wake me again at sunrise.

Dawn broke with an explosion of sound—not only prayer-callers, but roosters, street vendors, and people greeting each other in nearby courtyards. I quickly dressed and bounded down the stairs to breakfast.

A feast greeted me. It consisted of crusty bread, feta and kasseri cheeses, butter, honey, olives, yogurt, cucumbers, thick Turkish coffee, and a samovar filled with piping hot tea.

"*Günaydin,*" yelled out some the climbers.

"Güna-a-what?" I asked.

"Good morning. Günaydin means 'good morning,'" said Steve, the climber from Chicago. "Eat up," he continued. "You'll need lots of calories for the *dāg.*"

"What's a dãg?" I asked, laughing.

"Mountain," he replied. "Mountains eat up lots of calories."

Jack pulled up a chair and offered his own advice. "Before we head out of here, buy a couple bottles of water. You'll sweat water out until you dehydrate." He tied knots in a piece of rope and threw it at me. "Here's your water sling. Put a bottle in it, and carry it over your shoulder. Keep another bottle in your pack."

Water, or *su*, now became the topic of conversation. Jack had a filter to purify water. But we'd also have to fill bottles from streams. "How high up do we have to go before the water is pure?" asked an Oregon climber (and doctor) named Jay.

"Pretty high," responded Jack. "Herders take their cattle and sheep into the Alpine meadows. So human and animal feces get into the water until just about the snow line. You'll need to use my filter or drop in an iodine tablet."

Jack turned to me and asked, "Have you ever drunk iodine water? It doesn't taste great. When you buy your water, pick up some powdered juice mix."

Jay added his own advice: "Look for something with electrolytes in it—especially potassium and sodium. They wash out of your body with sweat. When you climb at altitude, lack of electrolytes can affect your mind."

As I got up from the breakfast table, I felt like I'd completed a class in basic mountaineering. "Set your watches," directed Jack. "We'll leave in about two hours."

The time passed quickly. About midmorning, nine of us

climbed aboard the bus. The group included seven climbers, Jack, and a Turkish mountain climber named Cemil. He pronounced his name for us—Jaa-MEAL. "If you can't remember this," said Cemil, "call me Jimmy." Then he made us say our names. I became D-bore-RAH.

The journey to the Pontic Mountains carried us almost completely across Turkey. First, we headed to Atatürk Airport. Here we hopped a plane to Ankara, the capital of Turkey. In Ankara, we took another plane to Erzurum on the eastern edge of the Anatolian Plateau. From here, we climbed into Land Rovers and headed north.

Cemil and Jack picked skilled drivers. They told us the drivers had experience dodging rockslides and herders. I thought they were joking until an avalanche of boulders crashed in front of us. A curse and a deft swerve of the wheel saved the vehicles. But it took our arms and backs to clear the road of debris.

Cemil's eyes sparkled as he looked at my sweat-and mud-covered clothes. "So, D-bore-RAH," he cackled, "Are we having fun yet?" Everybody started laughing.

"Another lesson, Deborah," chimed in Steve. "In mountain climbing, you get dirty. And, after days on the trail, you smell."

By the look of my clothes, the rockslide had given the dirt-and-smell process a head start. But, as people slapped my back, I felt part of the team. Together we got back into the Land Rovers and shared a treat—moist baby wipes. My sense of reality was beginning to change. The baby wipes felt like an extravagant luxury.

Six bone-jarring hours later, we arrived at the rushing waters of the Barhal Suyu River. Its source lay amid the glaciers and snowfields at the crest of the mountains. Cemil dared me to bathe. But I shivered just looking at the water. Instead, I went to look for a rock to urinate behind. "Hey, tourist," yelled Cemil. "Remember to burn your toilet paper. We don't want to litter our mountains." With the rock barely covering my backside, I muttered something about privacy, then scrambled back to camp.

The drivers pulled tents and cooking equipment from the Land Rovers. Then they left. We'd meet them after we climbed Mount Kackar.

As we put up the tents, I learned some mountain etiquette, or manners. Jack began, "I know you all know this, but. . ." Then came the rules. Don't wear boots inside your tent or someone else's tent. It makes a mess, and a pebble might tear a hole in the floor. Don't leave trash of any kind in camp or by the trail. Bury excrement. Don't trample the fragile environment. Bend a branch instead of breaking it. And don't "grunt," or rush, your way to the summit. Rushing makes you forget all the other rules. Plus it's dangerous.

Another lesson in basic mountaineering. I wrote everything down in a journal. Friends told me a journal would come in handy. "It will fill the evening hours," they said. But the journal forced me to do some soul-searching. At the end of this entry, I wrote: "I know so little."

Bizarre music in the distance forced me to snap my journal shut. It sounded like bagpipes. But we were in Turkey,

not Scotland. I stared in the direction of the music. Figures on horseback soon appeared. Sure enough, one of them was squeezing a set of bagpipes.

I had studied a lot of history. Yet I'd never read about bagpipe-playing Turks. "Who are they?" I asked Jack. He replied: "They're mountain people. They call themselves Laz. But they've got some Celtic in them. Probably some Mongol, too. I've hired them to carry our heavy gear from camp to camp."

So the mountains had a story to tell. And it was not just about rocks, peaks, and snow. Pockets of people—Laz, Hemsinli, Yuruk, Georgians, and more—kept alive traditions carried into the region by countless waves of invaders. I knew that the Celts settled in Scotland and Ireland. But how did they get to Turkey? "Simple," explained Cemil when I asked him this question. "They stopped off in Turkey on their way out of Asia." He winked, "It was so beautiful they decided to go no further." Well, that explained the bagpipes.

The horsemen set up camp next to ours. When the sun set, they built a huge bonfire. As the bagpipes wailed, the horsemen invited us to take part in a swirling circle dance called the Horon. One of the horsemen tied a yellow and red scarf around my head and pulled me into a circle. I can't dance. I'm not even coordinated. But that night I danced.

When the music stopped, I sat on the ground, exhausted. Suddenly a horseman set a gigantic hoop on fire. What now? I thought. The answer came in the form of pounding hooves. In one smooth motion, horse and rider glided through the hoop. "Mongols," I fantasized. "I bet that's what the Mongols looked like."

I stared at the mountains that ringed the camp. As the moon flickered on the peaks, I dreamed of the adventures ahead. "It can only get better," I smiled. It did. But not before it got a whole lot worse.

Sleep came quickly. So did morning. The clatter of pans and smell of food awakened me. The horsemen not only carried gear, they also cooked and boiled some hot water for a sponge bath. Given my growling stomach and filthy hands, I decided they must be angels in disguise.

Spirits ran high. We all wanted to start the climb. We wolfed down our food and packed up our gear. The weight of my load increased as I added food for lunch and bottles of water. The horsemen would use pack horses to haul the heaviest gear to the next camp.

My pack weighed about 18 pounds, and I felt in good shape. But I'd never climbed at altitude with weight on my back. Also, the thought of training hadn't even crossed my mind. The other climbers talked about running, biking, or hiking. Steve asked, "What exercise do you do?"

"Two or three times a week I jump on a stair machine for about 10 minutes," I replied. He gulped.

"That's it?"

Wide-eyed, I answered: "Sure. It's hard. I really have to breathe."

Nobody seemed to worry about my lack of gear. But the lack of training really concerned them. Who says I can't keep up with you? I thought. But this time, I really faced an uphill battle—seven miles worth of uphill battle. Our path would zigzag, with some level stretches. But in one day, we'd gain more than 2,000 feet in altitude. That meant thinner air and harder breathing.

I set out with my "Who says?" attitude. But, as the day wore on, my legs began to ache. Pain shot through muscles that I never knew existed. "Drink water," ordered Jack. "Muscles seize if they get dehydrated." If I stopped, other climbers said, "Don't rest too long. Your muscles will get cold and seize." When we finally paused for lunch, I collapsed. Just when I thought I could rest, Cemil said: "Time to give you some lessons in muscle stretching."

After lunch, the clouds began to thicken. Jack looked concerned as he picked up the pace. "Drill sergeant," I yelled at him.

"Deborah," he shot back. "Getting wet in the mountains is serious. Temperatures drop fast."

My rain gear was in my lost duffel bag. I moved too slowly. My muscles hurt. And I felt like crying. Mountain women don't cry, I thought.

When I glanced at Jack, he looked pretty miserable, too. He said, "It's my job to keep us safe. But I also want you to finish this climb. Let me take your pack."

I wanted to carry my weight. But I was too tired to protest. Only one word filled my mind—failure. It didn't cross my mind then that negative lessons can teach, too. In other words, I was learning that I'd have to train better for the next climb.

We made it to camp just one step ahead of a storm. We

took shelter in our tents as wind and rain battered the camp. The swaying tent made my heart race. I zipped open the flap a few inches to see if the stakes held. A gust of wind pulled open the flap, and a blast of rain soaked me. I felt a bone-chilling cold—and a sense of loneliness.

When the storm stopped, I emerged from the tent shivering. My walk seemed unsteady. "She's got hypothermia," someone yelled. Directions came fast. "Get out of your clothes." "Get into my sleeping bag, it's dry." "Let us hold you. You need our body warmth."

I forgot all body shame at this moment. I welcomed the dry clothes and comfort provided by my climbing partners. When I finally stopped shivering, Jack handed me a warm, sugary cup of tea. It was the best tea I've ever tasted in my life.

My bout with hypothermia—a body temperature below normal—had left me badly shaken. In near defeat, I decided to ask one of the horsemen to take me out of the mountains. But something amazing happened instead. A new horseman rode into camp. Out of a plastic sack, he pulled my lost duffel bag. The hotel had sent it by plane, bus, and horseback. Everybody clapped. "I guess you can't turn back now," smiled Jack.

"No, I guess I can't," I laughed.

The words "I can't" felt unfamiliar. I didn't use them much. But they sounded okay here in the mountains. Maybe I can't climb this mountain alone, I thought. But with the help of everyone else, I've got a shot.

The next few days followed a rhythm different from any

I had ever known. I got up with the sun and went to bed when it set. I let the contour of the land guide my walking. If I lagged behind, the mountains served as a map. "See the clump of trees at the top of that ridge," Jack might say. "We'll meet there for lunch."

The journey took me though many yaylas, or mountain villages. Sometimes women scolded me for not covering my arms or legs. So I stopped wearing T-shirts and shorts. Sometimes women descended from the Celts ran out with their light-haired sons or daughters. I let the children touch my own light hair. Once a group of women invited me to bathe with them in some hot springs. I gratefully accepted the offer. Through hand gestures, we shared our thoughts on marriage, children, and men.

The day eventually came when I reached the foot of Mount Kackar. This time I didn't choke back the tears. To be a mountaineer, you have to climb. And I was going to climb.

Mount Kackar is a Class 3 climb. That means, we didn't need ropes to climb the mountain. But there would be some exposure, or situations in which a climber steps into some pretty steep, open areas. To make it to the top in a single day, we'd have to start out at 4 A.M. with headlamps. So we all crawled into our sleeping bags early.

That night, I wrote in my journal: "I'm too excited to sleep. I've got to spend the night on the mountain." I put on some extra clothes and crept out of my tent. I made my way up the mountain to a point overlooking the camp. I propped myself up against a rock and watched the fog curl its way out of the valleys. It slowly snaked its way up to the camp and encircled the tents. Eventually, the fog slid up to my feet and covered me. The moonlight turned the fog into an silvery haze. I jumped up and hugged myself. Dancing around and around, I sang, "Climb away, Deborah, climb away."

As dawn approached, the fog started to curl back into the valleys. I glided back into camp. My watch showed 3:50 A.M. Jack and the other climbers greeted me. Moisture from the fog had dampened my clothes and hair. But I beamed. As I rambled on about the night, the other climbers recalled their first time on a mountain. We slapped on our backpacks and headed up.

Climbing tests your body. But it also tests your mind and spirit. Your muscles might scream, "Stop!" But your mind says, "Take just one more step." As the steps add up, your spirit soars. You spot something incredible and say, "I would have missed this if I had stopped." So you take another few steps.

Nobody had taught me this "walking meditation" yet. That would come on later climbs. But I must have practiced it on the Mount Kackar climb. I don't remember how my body felt. What I remember is the sight of pink rhododendrons next to a glacier. I also remember the sound of crunching snow beneath my feet. If I close my eyes, I still can feel the warm sun on my face.

Finally, we reached the summit. I now stood at the highest point in all of eastern Turkey. Small mountains and glaciers lay below us. To the north, I could see the Black Sea. It looked like a gemstone from this high up. After all the obstacles along the way, emotions overwhelmed me. I smiled and cried at the same time. I wanted to speak. But no words could express the experience. "Who could possibly understand my feelings?" I wondered to myself.

For an instant, I had forgotten the other climbers. As I looked around, I saw a mixture of reactions. Some stood in silence, their eyes fixed on some distant object. Big smiles crossed the faces of others. One smiling face gave me a thumbs-up signal with his hand. I had learned yet another lesson. Now I knew why such a close bond exists among climbers. We understand the one thing we cannot individually explain to nonclimbers—the emotions that lead us up the mountains.

I felt intensely tied to this group of people. Even though I might never see them again, I'd remember each one. At that minute, one of my climbing partners moved over to my side. "You'll never be the same," he said. "The magic of the mountains won't let you give them up. You'll be back. Maybe not here. But you'll be back in the mountains, probably sooner than you've imagined!"

I couldn't imagine another climb. Yet, after climbing Mount Kackar, I couldn't imagine *not* climbing. College and work had taken me from the cliffs in Hollowville, New York. But the desire to push new limits and to see the world from up high had never left me. "Yea," I said to the climber next to me. "I'll be back."

Today I know that Mount Kackar is not a hard mountain to climb. But it was my first. For that reason, the memory of the climb remains one of the most wonderful.

Aiming Higher

You never forget the click of a rifle bolt—especially when the rifle is pointed at you. It's even more riveting when the person holding the rifle doesn't speak English. There's no use running. So you hold up your hands, palms forward, hoping the person with the gun understands (and respects) the universal language of surrender.

I stumbled into a gun more than once after coming off Mount Kackar. The first time came when I prowled through a mountain village looking for a marketplace. Nobody had told me the village served as a military outpost. I was searching for fruit and vegetable stalls. But I found soldiers instead. Or, more accurately, they found me. I had just turned a corner when I found myself staring at a row of barracks. Out rushed a uniformed sentry with a gun aimed right at me. I threw up my hands and edged slowly back around the corner. Then I ran.

I raced out of breath into a tea shop. I was soaking with

sweat. Only then did I realize that the sweat from fear stinks a whole lot worse than the sweat from work. An English-speaking tea drinker asked, "Trouble, madam?" I blurted out what had happened. With a tired smile, he said, "The soldiers are necessary. Turkey has enemies along its eastern borders. There's a madman in Iraq. You know that, don't you?"

"Saddam Hussein," I replied. Yes, I knew about him. I'd even called the U.S. State Department before taking off. But it seemed unlikely that Hussein would attack Turkey. I told this to the tea drinker. He repeated, "Hussein's a madman."

I soon agreed. Two days' walk separated me from the mountains and a bus back to Erzurum. But now the mountain people had new stories to tell. They no longer cared about the color of my hair or eyes. The wanted me to carry a message back to America. Kurds, thousands of them, were fleeing Iraq. Hussein had used poison gas and bullets to drive them over the mountains into Turkey. Sorrow, instead of magic, now filled the mountains.

Jack and Cemil got us to the bus. But we ran into soldiers—and more rifles—along the way. The soldiers questioned us. Were we with the Central Intelligence Agency (CIA)? Were we reporters? If not, who were we?

I wanted to answer "we're climbers." But, under the circumstances, "American tourists" sounded a whole lot safer. I silently blessed the U.S. passport inside my fanny pack.

The passport satisfied the Turkish soldiers. However, it

provided flimsy protection against Iraqi terrorists. When the United States condemned Hussein's treatment of the Kurds, terrorists threatened to blow up U.S. planes leaving Turkey.

We had to board two flights to get home—one in Ankara and one in Istanbul. Turkish officials tried to thwart the terrorists. They canceled flights at the last minute and announced new ones. Specially trained dogs sniffed luggage for bombs. Every passenger, including me, submitted to a body search. Yet, each time a plane took off, I smelled the sweat of fear.

The worst fear came when we left Istanbul. Everybody held their breath as the plane nosed upward off the runway. Once airbound, one person started clapping, then another, and another. Soon applause filled the plane. An American exchange student next to me said, "I can't wait to be back in the U.S.A." I agreed. It was time to go home.

After the emotion-filled takeoff, the exchange student and I talked, first about the bomb threats and then about Turkey. "I came here to study Islamic culture," she said. "Why did you come?"

"To climb a mountain," I replied. The words felt good coming out of my mouth—so good that I spilled out the whole Mount Kackar story. At the end of the tale, she remarked: "I never met a mountaineer before. It sounds exciting."

My seatmate's comment set off a whole chain of thoughts. How could I be a mountaineer? I'd only climbed one mountain. What did I know about mountaineering?

Not much, I told myself. Did I have the "right stuff" to even dream about becoming a mountaineer? I loved the mountains. Was that enough? Maybe if I traveled with men who'd help me. But I didn't want to rely on men. This five foot three inch, 110-pound woman wanted to do it on her own.

I might not know a lot about mountaineering, but I'd already figured out that a woman faced some special problems on the mountains. Privacy is one. How does a woman bathe or urinate? She can duck behind a tree or rock. But trees disappear at high altitudes, and rocks aren't always around. So I learned to use a poncho—or a big skirt—like a tent. (Imagine a lily pad floating in a pond. That's what my Turkish porters said I looked like when I wore my poncho to wash up in a lake.)

Menstruation is another problem. In some parts of the developing world, it's taboo—or forbidden by one's culture—for men to be around women when they have their period. A Turkish porter refused to carry my gear when he discovered a tampon in a latrine. And, remember you're not supposed to litter the mountains. So women need to carry small shovels to bury tampons or carry them out with other garbage.

There's also the matter of physical strength. On many mountains, porters carry gear part of the way. But on the highest ascents, mountaineers carry their own equipment, including oxygen tanks, if necessary. True, they sometimes drag their gear on sleds, while they try to ski or snowshoe forward. Still it's hard enough for a man to lug 60-80 pounds—whether it be on his back or on a sled. What about a small woman like me? Did she even have a hope of carrying her own weight?

I crunched up my shoulders at this last question. An 18-pound pack had felt heavy on the Mount Kackar climb. I shuddered at the thought of lugging more than half my weight up a mountain. (My poor aching back.) And suppose I had to trudge through knee-deep snow? (Now my leg muscles throbbed.) Or suppose I had to haul the pack up a wall of rock or ice. (There go my arm muscles.) Just imagining the climb made me feel exhausted.

Overwhelming odds—small woman in her late thirties tackles big mountain. It sounded like a major challenge. But the old "who says" attitude started working its magic. I smiled, *Who says I can't become a mountaineer?*

After I got home, I shared my dream. Some people thought I'd lost my mind. (Actually, what they said was, "Are you crazy?") I decided to search for other women climbers who shared my insanity. I started in the libraries. Here I turned up Julia Archibald Holmes. In 1858, Julia put on a pair of bloomers and climbed Pike's Peak—all 14,110 feet! Using a rock as a writing desk, Julia wrote: "Nearly everyone tried to discourage me from this task. But I believed that I should succeed. . . . In all probability, I am the first woman to reach this summit."

The bookstores offered thin encouragement. Books specifically about or by women climbers did not begin to appear until 1990. So I hit the climbing stores. If I spotted a woman, I talked with her, asking her to share stories or advice. One gave me a tip. She said, "There's not a lot written about us yet. But check the August 1987 issue of *Climbing*. It's all about women." Back at the library, I photocopied the cover. When faced with doubters, I could wave it and say, "We exist."

A year passed. But the magic of the mountains didn't fade. I pored over travel brochures looking for a place where people lived and talked mountains. One place turned up time and time again—Nepal, the home of Mount Everest.

Even today, only about six hundred people have climbed to the top of Everest, the tallest mountain on the planet. But each year dozens of people try. More often than not, they're driven off by 100-mile-per-hour winds or blinding snowstorms. Some climbers wait out the storms in snow caves. But if a storm lasts more than a week, the thin air and frozen temperatures will drive them down. Climbers who miss or survive the storms still face killer avalanches and deadly crevasses. Some crevasses, gaping cracks in the glaciers, are exposed. Others lay hidden beneath the snow waiting to swallow climbers.

Nobody needed to tell me to stay off Everest. But I still wanted to see it. I also wanted to learn more about the Himalayas. Running from the edge of China to the edge of Pakistan, these peaks drew climbers like magnets. I wondered if their magnetism would attract or repel me.

In 1991, I decided to find out. As a single woman, I wanted time to learn how to get around Nepal on my own. So I signed up for an Earthwatch project.

(Earthwatch sponsors researchers interested in studying our planet.) I chose to work on a farming project in Phaplu, a village northeast of Kathmandu, the capital of Nepal. Phaplu lay at about 8,000 feet. Two week's work at altitude would prepare me to climb higher. I already had a route in mind. From Phaplu, you can trek to the bases of two mountains—Annapurna and Everest.

Memories of the Mount Kackar climb guided my preparations. I needed bigger trekking boots. Coming down Mount Kackar my feet jammed forward so often that I lost most of my toenails. Crippling blisters taught me that the boots needed to be broken in, too. Nobody needed to remind me about hypothermia. I selected fabrics that would wick—absorb moisture and dry quickly. I also bought heavy-duty rain gear and thermal underwear. (I've learned to love thermals—lightweight, midweight, expedition weight, all weights.)

While shopping in a climbing store, the clerk talked me into buying *Messner: All 14 Eight-Thousanders*. The book told the story of Reinhold Messner, the mountaineer who climbed all fourteen of the world's 8,000 meter peaks. (A meter equals roughly three feet. So an 8,000 peak is more than 24,000 feet.)

"He did it without oxygen tanks," said the clerk. Then with a sparkle in his eye, he asked: "Do you know how Reinhold toughens his hands for rock climbing?" Before I could reply, the clerk answered his own question. "He rubs them with ice chips and gravel."

With a grimace, I replied, "Very macho. Do you think a

woman would do that?"

He laughed, "Do you think a woman would climb Everest?" Neither of us knew that Stacy Allison (a five foot three inch, 110-pound woman) had just become the first U.S. woman to reach Everest's summit.

My twenty-six-hour flight to Nepal carried me more than halfway around the world. Stops included Seattle, Hong Kong, Bangkok (Thailand), and finally Kathmandu. En route, I tried to imagine the people of Nepal. I'd seen their faces in guide books—Hindu holy men named *sadhus*, Buddhist priests called *lamas*, and Sherpas, the mountain people who lived in the shadow of the Himalayas. I closed my eyes and held imaginary conversations with the faces. I tried to talk in Nepali. "*Namaste*," I said. It meant, literally, "I greet the god within you." Then I imagined Mount Everest. I whispered, "Namaste, Mount Everest."

Getting Hooked

"Ka-Ka-Ka-Kathmandu. That's really where I'm going to. When I get outta of here, I'm going to Kathmandu." The lyrics never came out right. Neither did the melody. But I still couldn't get the words from Bob Seger's rock song, "Kathmandu," out of my mind. In the fall of 1991, I really was going to Kathmandu. But what did I actually know about the city except that it was one of the most faraway places somebody in the United States could head to?

I decided to look up information on Kathmandu in books. I found out that the city lay along The Silk Road, an ancient trade route that connected the silk markets of China with the spice markets of India. I also found out that snow rarely falls in the city. Even at an elevation of 4,500 feet, Kathmandu lies snugly tucked in a valley. In winter, howling winds slam into the Himalayas and drop their snow. While blizzards rage in the mountains, marigolds and roses bloom in the valley below.

My guide book said about 235,000 people lived in Kathmandu. But the guide book never prepared me for their variety. My first walk through the narrow, dusty city streets astonished me. On one corner, a woman lit a candle to honor a Hindu god. On another, a Buddhist monk spun a prayer wheel. In one doorway, a beggar held out a rice bowl. In another, a merchant sold vegetables. The city felt like a giant kaleidoscope. Every time I turned, I saw a new pattern—a new set of faces, new ways of life.

I traveled to Kathmandu at the start of a five-day festival called Tihaar. Although Tihaar is a Hindu festival, most Nepalis take part in it, including Buddhists. During the first four days, the Nepalis honor animals with spiritual importance. Crows receive dishes of grain. Dogs and cows wear garlands of marigolds. Bullocks wander the streets with horns covered in silver and gold foil. On the last day of the festival, sisters honor their brothers with presents.

On the final night, the city explodes with celebration. Dance troupes from the Kathmandu Valley swirl through the streets. Fireworks shoot up from the roofs. Lamps flicker from homes—beacons to guide the souls of the newly departed to heaven. Incense fills the air. So does laughter.

At first, I watched the celebration from my hotel with the rest of the Earthwatch team. "What do you think?" asked Dan, the team leader. "Do you wanna plunge in?" We ran into the streets and let the crowds sweep us away.

The next morning, we boarded a sixteen-seat propeller plane bound for Phaplu. The flight carried us into Khumbu, the Sherpa region nearest to Mount Everest.

From the window, the rugged landscape looked like a giant maze of valleys and mountains. To land, we flew directly into the maze.

Dan had warned us about the landing. "It's like setting down inside a bowl," he had said. And it was. The pilot flew through a break in the mountains and dropped fast. He then headed toward a short dirt runway in one of the valleys. If he overshot the runway, we'd crash into a deeper valley. If he tried to pull out, we risked smacking into a mountain. It was definitely a fear-sweat landing.

Once in Phaplu, Dan went over the project. He wanted to study cultivation of a grain called amaranth. Scientists had thought amaranth was native to the Andes of South America. Its cultivation in the Himalayas had startled them. "It's a mystery," said Dan. "How did amaranth managed to jump halfway around the world? And where did it grow first—the Andes or the Himalayas?" He also wanted to teach the Sherpas to grow more of this nutritious grain. Aside from popping it for snacks or brewing it as tea, the Sherpas included almost no amaranth in their diets.

Dan assigned jobs based on our résumés and interests. I drew the job of interviewer. Along with a sixteen-year-old translator named Konjo, I would live and work with a Sherpa woman named Sena Lama.

Sena Lama knew how to climb. In fact, she climbed every day. Smaller and a lot older than me, Sena scrambled up the steep trails to her field. My altitude watch said we gained 1,000 feet each morning. Not used to the altitude, I breathed more heavily than her. Seeing my discomfort, Sena would say, "*Bistaari, bistaari.*" ("Go slowly, slowly.") I'd eye the woven, tool-filled basket on her back, and say: "*Tyaki laagyo?*" ("Aren't you tired?") A smile would cross her creased face, and we'd start walking.

With Konjo's help, I learned a lot about the *Sherpanis*, or Sherpa women. Among other things, they knew about the mountains. Sena told me stories about famous Sherpa porters and guides. She had also traveled the routes to Annapurna and Everest herself. I pulled out a map and asked Sena to show me the way. She moved her finger along trails, describing each bazaar or monastery.

The routes involved a lot of trekking, some of it at 18,000 feet. I asked Konjo if Sena thought I'd make it. The two women talked in Sherpa and started laughing.

"What's so funny," I asked.

Konjo replied, "Sena says you can do it. But she thinks maybe you'd walk a lot faster if a lama promised to find you a husband in the mountains." That remark kicked off a whole new discussion. Which was better: Sherpa arranged marriages or love marriages like those in the United States? We argued and laughed before curling up on the sleeping mats. As I closed my eyes, Konjo said: "Don't worry, our friend R.P. will get you to the mountains—without a husband."

Nearly everyone in Phaplu knew R.P. His family owned a lot of timberland. Once cut for fuel and building, forests had become scarce in Khumbu. People faced arrest if they cut a living tree or branch without a permit. Ownership of forested land made R.P. a *thulo maanchhe*—a big man.

But people respected R.P. for more than his land. According to Buddhist tradition, well-to-do families sent their second sons to monasteries. Over the generations, R.P.'s family had produced many *rinpoches*, or lamas of high standing. (Rinpoche means "Precious One.") Although R.P. was not a lama, he knew many important Buddhist leaders, including the Dalai Lama—the head of Tibetan Buddhism.

People also respected R.P. for another reason. As a youth, he had worked as a high-altitude porter and guide. He eventually rose to *sirdar*, the chief Sherpa on an expedition. On five separate occasions, R.P. lugged tents, equipment, and 18-pound oxygen tanks up Mount Everest. Once he made it all the way to Camp 4, at 26,000 feet. Then the oxygen ran low. The *bideshi*, or foreigners, who had hired the Sherpas got first shot at the summit. Although R.P. had used no oxygen thus far, he remained behind. The last push might require oxygen, and there was none to spare.

I knew all this about R.P. even before I met him. He also knew all about me. Phaplu had no electric lines, no telephones, and no TVs. Yet news traveled fast. People loved to gossip at tea shops. They greeted each other on the trails with a string of questions: "Where are you coming from?" "What's new there?" "Where are you going?" "Who will you see?" "Will you carry a message for me?"

One evening, Konjo walked with me to visit R.P. His wife seated us in places of honor by the fire and served cups of *chaii*, or milk tea. We talked for a while. Then R.P.

said, "You have questions, Deborah?"

"Yes, R.P., I want to know how you felt about not making it up Everest."

He drew a breath and said: "The Sherpas call Everest *Chomolungma*, 'mother goddess of the earth.' It is enough that I was with her. It is enough that I tried."

"Will you try again?" I asked.

R.P. glanced over at his young son and daughter. "No," he responded. "My path is now with my family, not the mountains."

"Now I have a question, Deborah," said R.P. "Where does your path carry you?"

"I'm not sure," I answered. "But I think it carries me to the mountains, on a journey you've already traveled."

He looked at me, and asked, "Will you meet me before sunrise tomorrow? We will wear headlamps and walk to a point high above Phaplu. If it is clear, you will see the sun rise on the summit of Chomolungma."

I barely slept that night. When my alarm went off at 3:30 A.M., I flew to meet R.P. He held a gift for me, a string of wooden beads. "They're called *malas*," explained R.P. "There's 108 of them. You hold them in your hand, and turn each bead one at a time. Every time you turn a bead, you say the words *Om mani padme hum*."

"Hail to the jewel in the lotus." It was a phrase sacred to Buddhism, a request to be one with the universe. I wondered why R.P. was telling me this now. He saw the confused look on my face. "When I climb, I meditate," said R.P. "It keeps my mind and heart at peace. Carry the malas with you into the mountains so you can learn to walk through fear with peace."

"*Dhanyabaad*," I said softly. "Thank you, for the gift."

R.P. smiled, "Let's practice your walking meditation. It's still dark, so watch the trail with your headlamp. With each step breathe slowly. Or, if you like, turn the malas."

We walked quietly most of the way. But every now and then R.P. gave me some advice. When we came to snow, he taught me how to "snow walk." With each step, I dug the heel of my boot into the snow, then stepped forward. This goose-steplike strut kept me from slipping backward.

Another time, R.P. talked about altitude. "Thin air makes people a little crazy," he said. "They get angry." He then stopped to make a point. "If you put a 'd' in front of anger, do you know what you get? D–A–N–G–E–R. Anger is dangerous." His words come back to me whenever I lose my temper—especially on a climb.

Around 6:00 A.M., the sky lightened. Frost and snow covered everything, including me. We stopped in a clearing at the top of a ridge. R.P. motioned to a bank of clouds in the distance. "Watch over there," he said. I kept my eyes glued to the clouds. In my pocket, I turned the *malas*, one by one. Slowly, the clouds began to move. "There it is," called out R.P. "There's Everest."

I ran over to R.P. almost at the same moment the snow-clad summit appeared. Overpowering in its beauty, Everest seemed to float in the sky. It hung there for about a half hour before the clouds reembraced it. I turned to R.P. and said, "I've got to get closer to the mountains. Can you help me?"

R.P. arranged for everything—permits, gear, and a young Sherpa guide named Norbu. We traveled first to Annapurna, part by open-air truck and part by foot. Along the way, I stayed in thatched tea houses, trekking lodges, and monasteries. I ate endless *chapattis* (flatbreads) and bowls of *daal* (lentil soup).

Finally, I arrived in Chomrong, the highest village on the final stretch into Annapurna. That night, I shared a table with a group of Australians. They told one climbing story after the other. I laughed and learned. But I wished out loud for more stories of my own. "Then keep on climbing," said a trekker named Ken. "The mountains teach you stories you've never even dreamed of."

The next day proved him right. I entered the Annapurna Sanctuary, an oval amphitheater three miles wide. Rising directly from its walls soared nine peaks over 21,000 feet high. From their summits spilled cascades of glacial ice. People climb those peaks, I said to myself. In fact, Annapurna—the peak that gave the amphitheater its name—was the first "eight-thousander" ever climbed. Norbu seemed to read my mind. "Want to try them?" he asked. "Not yet," I laughed.

While Norbu prepared to head off for Everest, I stared at the mountains. I let my mind carry me into their icy beauty. The thought of climbing glaciers overwhelmed me. Then I recalled a remark by a mountaineer named Max Stirner. "The more we know of something," said Stirner, "the smaller appear those obstacles that at first seemed insurmountable." As I left to join Norbu, I muttered, "Well, Deb, I guess you'll have to learn all about glaciers. Then maybe those icy obstacles will seem a little smaller."

We set out once again by truck and by foot. The journey to Everest led through mountain villages and up steep trails to *gompas*, or Buddhist monasteries. (Gompa literally means "high place.") I traced our route on the map as we got closer to Namche Bazaar, the unofficial capital of Khumbu. Traders came from as far as Tibet to sell their goods at Namche. The town also served as one of the last stopping points for expeditions heading up Everest.

By the time I wandered into Namche, I knew that nature had given me a gift. I handled altitude well. I had spent weeks trudging between 9,000 and 17,000 feet. Signs of altitude sickness never appeared. No headaches, no nausea, no sleeplessness. Now I wanted, more than anything, to see Everest up close. So Norbu and I decided to push up the trail, rather than stay in Namche.

Three nights later, we slept on the sod floor of a tea house less than eight hours away from Kala Patar, or the "Black Rock." From its 18,192-foot crest, the entire south face of Everest can be seen. "We'll start the ascent before dawn," said Norbu.

"The sooner the better," I replied.

The alarm on my watch sent us fumbling in the dark for our gear. We headed out with headlamps, but the sun soon edged up. As we climbed, Norbu pointed to a hillside dotted with dozens of rock shrines called *churungs*. "They honor the Sherpas who have died on the mountain," he explained. Looking at the piles of stone, I remembered the string of beads that R.P. had given me. I took off one of the beads and placed it among the churungs. "It is correct," said Norbu.

By late morning, we reached the top of Kala Patar. As I raised my eyes up to the world's tallest mountain, I pressed the palms of hands together. With a slight bow, I whispered, "Namaste, Mount Everest. At last we meet." Surveying the surrounding peaks, I said out loud: "The name Chomolungma suits you well."

"What?" asked Norbu.

"She really is the mother goddess of the earth," I replied. "Look at how all the other peaks bow down to her."

Norbu laughed. "And you, Deborah, how do you feel about our mother goddess?" I thought, I feel humbled, not just by the mountain but by the people who have risked their lives to touch her face.

Looking up at the summit some 10,000 feet away, I knew that I also wanted to touch the faces of mountains. I might not ever climb Everest, but I'd climb whatever mountain I could. Maybe I wouldn't reach all the summits. But what was a summit anyway? Nothing more than a few square feet of rock or snow. I remembered what R.P. had said about not reaching the top of Everest. "It is enough that I tried." I decided my only failure would be *not* to try.

As I headed down Kala Patar, I made myself a promise. Rock climbing, ice climbing, high-altitude climbing—I'd do it all. And, in trying, I'd meet myself—the woman who loved saying "Who says?"

Body, Mind, and Soul

I can almost see the question coming. People have asked it hundreds of times. The minute I hear the "Why," I can finish the question for them: ". . . do I climb?"

I struggle for an answer. Out of kindness to friends and loved ones, I give reasons that nonclimbers will understand. "It's the beauty of the mountains." "It's the adventure." "It's the need to be nearer to angels."

But these answers are only partially true, except for maybe the last one. I started searching for angels as a little girl. So my family and longtime friends accept my story about looking for them in the mountains. (In fact, my mother has given me a small angel to carry with me.) What most nonclimbers have a harder time accepting is another more complicated answer: "I climb for the fear."

As any mountaineer knows, fear helps keep you alive. Mountains don't bow easily to conquest. They humble even the proudest, strongest climber. They play no favorites. High-altitude mountain climbing is dangerous. The climber who does not experience fear invites disaster. As my friend Dan says: "There are old climbers. And there are bold climbers. But there are no bold, old climbers."

On a challenging climb, fear talks to me a lot. It asks: "What's really important to you, Deb?" Things that seemed like mountains at home—jobs, bills, a broken heart— become tiny. Fear puts my life in focus. I take joy in a hot meal, a warm facecloth, or a clean pair of socks.

Fear also dares me to call its bluff. "Back down," it says. "Not yet," I reply. "You can't make it," whispers the fear. "We'll see," I laugh. With the battle lines drawn, I push my physical strength and courage to the limit. I test my muscles, my climbing skills, and sometimes my luck. I feel immense freedom when I win. "Another fear knocked down!" I exclaim. If the fear proves stronger, my instincts take over. "It's too much of a risk," warns my gut. "Try it later." And usually I do. Fear is a great motivator. It makes me want to learn how to beat it.

Climbers have their own *why* question. If some of us need fear, why don't others? Some people say climbers are adrenaline junkies—people addicted to the rush of a chemical (adrenaline) secreted by the body when emotions run high. If you've ever experienced fear, you know that it's certainly an intense emotion. But even more intense—and addictive—is the peace that comes from facing your fears. Many mountaineers go to the mountain to conquer themselves, not the mountain.

So just how do you prepare to conquer yourself on a

mountain? You embark on a three-part training program that involves the body, mind, and soul. Each person brews up her or his own equation for mixing these elements. Here's my equation.

Mountaineering requires good conditioning, especially for a small woman like me. When I decided to jump into mountaineering, I promised to jump into a gym. My experience on Mount Kackar had taught me the importance of training. But I didn't want to become a muscle-bound "iron rat," somebody who pumps up until they look like the Hulk. Other climbers advised me to develop a good strength-to-weight ratio. "Every pound of muscle means another pound to lug up a mountain," said one climber in Nepal. The climber then looked me over from head to toe and added: "But you should bulk up a little for those 50- to 60-pound packs. Five to 10 pounds maybe. That should increase your strength by almost ten percent."

I also needed to learn how to breathe. Simple, you might say. But at altitude, breathing becomes harder and harder. (I've come to appreciate the oxygen-rich environment of my sea-level home in Wiccopee, New York.) So in addition to weight training, there's cardiovascular training—biking, running, swimming, and jumping rope.

I walked into the gym with firm intentions to put muscle behind my dreams. But the sight of a weight room full of iron-pumping, sweating, grunting men sent me flying into the Nautilus room. Here, well-toned women dressed in lycra tights stopped me dead in my tracks. To train, it seemed, I had to conquer my own body hang-ups. I thought, Well, Deb, if you want to climb mountains, you'll just have to let people see your puny little self.

So, with all the low self-esteem you can imagine, I stripped off my bulky sweatshirt and stepped onto a treadmill. Instead of thinking about my physical shape, I dreamed of mountains. I caught my stride on the treadmill, pushed up the speed and incline, and pretended each step carried me toward a peak.

Lost in sweat and daydreams, I forgot everybody else in the gym until a voice snapped me back to reality. "Knock, knock, anybody in there?" said the voice. "Hey, you, can you hear me?" It took a few seconds to attach a face to the voice. As my daydream faded, my friend Barbara appeared. "Whew," she said, "I thought we'd lost you."

Barbara works in the gym as a trainer. Our paths crossed when I first wandered into the gym in 1989. But I didn't stay long. My commitment to climbing wasn't strong enough to overcome my dislike of rooms full of people. Even in junior high and high school, I dreaded gym class. I wandered off alone whenever possible. The only sports I liked were solitary sports—swimming, running, biking, and the trampoline. No wonder I took so quickly to mountaineering. I loved the time alone.

"What are you doing here?" Barbara asked.

"I'd rather be anyplace else," I admitted. "But I need to build up my endurance. And I don't have a clue on where to begin."

"Want me to help you?" Barbara smiled.

"What do you know about training mountain climbers?"

I laughed.

"If they're athletes," replied Barbara, "I know how to train them."

So I started a training program that lasted for two years. Correct training takes patience. Results don't come overnight. Sometimes it involves a lot more toil than joy. Barbara and I developed a routine. I complained: "It's too hard." "I'm too tired." "I don't like this exercise." She'd respond: "Waa! Waa! Waa! Quit your crying. You want to get up those mountains, don't you?"

Eventually, I learned enough to take over my own training. I set up a mini-gym in the dining room of my old farmhouse. It includes a stair machine, free weights, a jump rope, and a small nautilus. I work out four to six times a week under the watchful supervision of my five dogs. Like some of my friends, they haven't a clue as to why I do this. But I know. It helps me get up mountains.

It would take another book to describe specific training exercises. There's calisthenics: dips, pull-ups, push-ups, and sit-ups. And these calisthenics vary. There's a half dozen ways to do sit-ups. Each one works a different set of muscles. (People breathe from the abdomen. So a "good center" is important to climbing.)

Weight training also helps me. Quadriceps, hamstrings, biceps, triceps, latissimus dorsi("lats"), pectorals ("pecs")— these and other muscles get worked out every week. I concentrate on my legs—the pistons that pump my body up the mountains. But I don't neglect my back and shoulders. They need to support packs and hold my weight if I grab onto a rock to pull myself over a boulder or ledge.

Every climber needs a strong heart and good lungs. So I regularly run or climb on the stair machine. Some winter mornings, I look out at the frost and groan, "It's too cold to run." Then I think of the cold air that will fill my lungs on the mountains. I pull on my thermals, a face mask, and gloves. Then I head out to sprint between telephone poles. Neighbors have now joined the list of people who ask: "Why?"

At the end of every workout, I stretch. Stretching not only feels good, it increases flexibility. Scrambling up a mountain sometimes can require incredible moves. Perched on a ledge hundreds of feet off the ground, you face a decision: back down or make that high reach or step. Most climbers go for the stretch.

The decision to push on to the next level goes beyond the body. An unseen, but deeply felt, mental and spiritual power whispers, "Go for it!" In that split second, thoughts of success or failure vanish. All that matters is the effort— a chance to try. As my friend Em says, "It's better to try and fail, than not to try at all."

These are the words of encouragement that feed the mind and spirit. At more than seventy years old, Em still hikes and rides a motorbike. She also supports my climbing. "Young lady," says Em, "don't let anybody talk you out of those mountains. You've still got a whole life ahead of you. Live it."

You can't climb if the body doesn't work. But, for me, the mind also has to be in shape. That means a good mental attitude. None of my family or friends climb. So it's up to me to keep the enthusiasm alive. I read about climbing, talk about climbing, and call people who climb in other parts of the United States. Today a week rarely passes without someone asking: "How's the training going?" "Where's the next mountain?" Questions like these fuel my excitement. I've started to believe that nonclimbers actually like all my stories. Even my mother shares my pictures with her friends. "Do you know what Deb did now?" she asks them.

Yet, when I'm alone, nagging doubts creep in. Mountaineering gear requires money. So do guides and teachers. I worked long hours to buy the necessary equipment—down sleeping bag, arctic parka, bib overalls, ice boots, snowshoes, expedition backpack, and more. I saved to afford teachers. I still save for trips. Then I give up assignments to go on a climb. As I struggle to meet the bills, I wonder: "Did I make the right choice? Should I be living a more normal life?"

At these times, I rebuild my mental attitude by sharing my hopes and fears with a couple of longtime friends— Fran, Susan, Francie, Charity, Dan, and Rich. They get the late night or early morning phone calls. They hear about my financial worries.

"Don't listen to those fears," advises Susan. "I'll be the first to call you with work."

"I won't let you be a bag lady," laughs Francie.

They listen to my flights of fancy and talk of even bigger mountains.

"Hang onto those dreams," says Fran.

"Keep talking to the angels," encourages Charity.

They support my habit.

"You know that gear you wanted," asks Rich. "Well, I bought it for you."

They place their confidence in me.

"Get up that mountain," Dan tells me as I head out. "You're climbing for all of us."

For an ordinary, amateur climber like me, this handful of friends boosts me over the rough spots. But each time I head out, I head out alone. Here's where the spiritual training pays off. Before a climb, I increase my meditation. I envision the mountain. I talk to it. I live in two worlds. My body performs everyday tasks. But my spirit already has taken the first steps up the mountain. It's my scout. From some faraway place, it beckons, "It's a great journey. Catch up with me."

In 1992, my spirit-scout carried my imagination to the tallest mountain in Africa—Mount Kilimanjaro. I started to dream about it. Then I turned the dream into reality. As soon as I bought a ticket, all doubts about climbing vanished. They always do. I felt like I was going home.

Tropical Ice

Magic exists on the East African savanna. It exists in the vast stretches of sweeping brown grasses. It exists in the immense beasts—elephant, giraffe, and rhino—that stride through the grasses. It exists in the swirling dust clouds kicked up by the hooves of wildebeest or zebra as they flee a pride of lions. It exists in the blazing sunsets that illuminate the twisted and thorned acacia trees. It exists in Kilimanjaro, a mountain that rises out of the savanna and floats in the sky like a huge white-capped blue wave.

Kilimanjaro is a brash, young mountain by East African standards. Most of the region's volcanoes burst on the scene some ten million years ago. At that time, the African continent began to rip apart as two great plates beneath the earth's crust shifted. The ground between these plates collapsed, creating a deep scar. The scar—known today as the Great Rift Valley—runs all the way from the Gulf of Suez in the north to the nation of Malawi in the south.

The movement of the plates created awesome explosions on the surface. Great cones of lava thrust skyward. The lava built up layer by layer, leaving scattered volcanoes throughout Ethiopia, central Kenya, and western Uganda. Over the millenniums, the forces of erosion wore down these peaks. When movement of the plates spit up Mount Kilimanjaro some one million years ago, it stood taller than any volcano on the continent.

This volcanic youngster defies geography. Imagine a glacier-clad mountain two hundred miles from the equator. Also imagine temperatures that range from 100° F at the mountain's base to –20° F at the summit. Then imagine a crater 19,340 feet above sea level with fumes of sulfur leaking out from holes in the crater's surface. Now you have a picture of Mount Kilimanjaro—the largest freestanding mountain in the world.

When German missionary Johannes Rebmann first described Kilimanjaro in 1848, skeptics in Britain's Royal Geographic Society hooted in disbelief. Scoffed one official: "Statements such as these betray weak powers of observation, strong fancy, and an eager childish craving for wonder."

The official probably wasn't a mountain climber. "An eager childish craving for wonder." It's a perfect reason for climbing a mountain, especially when the mountain is covered with tropical ice.

Guided by a "craving for wonder," I set out for Kilimanjaro in September 1992. On my airline ticket, I wrote a phrase from Ernest Hemingway's short story, "The

Snows of Kilimanjaro." It read: "larger than life and white as snow." I also jotted down the way the Chagga who live on the mountain's eastern edge spell it: Kilima Njaro. Below this spelling, I wrote three different English translations of the mountain's name: "white mountain," "shining mountain," and "mountain of springs." Just before landing in Moshi, Tanzania, the pilot announced: "Out the window to your right, folks, you can get a real nice view of Kilimanjaro." As I looked out the window, I added another word to my ticket: *magic!*

As "oohs" and "ahs" filled the plane, a little girl leaned over and asked: "Who lives there?"

"Angels," I replied. She looked back out the window. The broad dome wore a halo of clouds. The glacial ice sparkled. "I'm going to climb that mountain," I said.

The little girl turned to me and asked, "Will you tell the angels hello?"

With a smile, I answered, "You bet!"

I reached inside the travel pouch that hung from my neck and took out an amethyst crystal that my friend Charity had given me. "Carry this and think of me, the angels, or whatever else will protect you," Charity had said. I handed it to the little girl. "An angel gave it to me," I told her.

"Will the angels give you another one on the mountain?" she asked.

"I think so," I responded.

My travels abroad had taught me not to rely on English. Out of necessity and respect for other cultures, I learned key phrases to get around without a translator. As our plane prepared for landing, I practiced a few phrases in Swahili, the universal language of East Africa. With dozens of languages in the region, Swahili makes it possible for the people of East Africa to talk to each other. I hoped it would get me around, too. I whispered some greetings to the window. "*Habari* means hello." "So does *jambo*." "*Nzuri* means fine." "*Asante* means thank you." "*Kwa heri* means good-bye." "And if somebody calls me *mama*, it's okay. It's a sign of respect for an adult woman."

As the wheels of the plane hit the runway, I repeated a Swahili proverb: "*Haba na haba hujaza kibaba*." "Little and little fill the kibaba-measure." It meant, "Doing things a little bit at a time will get you where you want to be." Where I wanted to be was the top of Kilimanjaro. Little by little, one step after the other, I hoped to make it.

The first steps involved getting through the chaos of Kilimanjaro International Airport. A swarm of people, mostly East Africans, pressed in from all sides. I grasped my inoculation card tightly. Rumor said officials gave shots if you couldn't prove immunization against contagious diseases such as yellow fever. The threat of epidemics haunt developing nations such as Tanzania. Tourist traffic from other lands means traffic in diseases, too.

I also had to protect myself against diseases no longer common in the United States. I had shots against polio, meningococcus, typhoid, cholera, and yellow fever. I also took a vaccination against hepatitis A, gotten from impure water and food. And I took a series of three shots against hepatitis B, contracted from impure blood. My mother, who is a nurse, didn't like to think of me falling. "If you hurt yourself," she warned, "you might need blood. Please protect yourself." Finally, I carried malaria pills in case I traveled into a mosquito-infested area in the rain forests or along the coast.

With inoculation card in hand, I headed toward immigrations. As the immigration official checked over the card, I remarked: "I feel like a walking medicine cabinet." He didn't laugh.

"You're lucky your country has this kind of medicine," he said with a steely gaze. "Some people in Tanzania are not so fortunate."

I felt ashamed at my flip remark. Seeing my discomfort, the official made a suggestion. "Want to help us?" he asked. "Then leave behind some of the medicines that you Americans carry. Give them to a local clinic in some village before you leave."

From behind me, a voice said: "Sounds like good advice. I think I'll take it, too." I turned around to see a thin gray-haired man in trekking boots. "Where are you headed?" he asked.

"Kilimanjaro," I responded.

"Me, too," he replied. "You wouldn't be going with the group that pioneered the Shira route, would you?"

I blurted out, "Wow! I can't believe it. I am." With a big smile and an outstretched hand, he introduced himself.

"Hi, I'm Bill. I climb mountains, sky dive, tell bad jokes, and help blond women find clinics to donate their medical supplies." Even the immigration official smiled.

"Get out of here," he directed. "And keep your promise about the medicines—both of you."

"Where do you come from?" I asked Bill. My heart leaped when he answered, "Kansas." "Great," I replied. "It's a flat state. You'll have as much trouble clawing your way to altitude as me."

He started laughing. "Sorry to disappoint you. But I've weathered blizzards on Mount McKinley and trekked all 23,085 feet up Mount Aconcagua."

With a twinge of envy, I shot back, "So, you've climbed the two highest peaks in the Western Hemisphere. What other notches have you carved on your ice ax?"

"When we're on Kili, remind me to tell you about skydiving off Angel Falls in Venezuela or bungee jumping in Australia," he replied.

I slipped my hand around Bill's arm. "So what are you?" I asked. "Some kind of professional daredevil?"

He laughed again. "Nope. Lawyer by trade, churchgoer by weekend, husband and father by night. I only do the daredevil stuff part-time."

As we talked, Bill and I spotted five other would-be climbers. The boots and backpacks gave them away. "They're probably the rest of the Shira group," I said.

A tousled, dark-haired man waved to us. "I'm Wesley," he shouted out, "your guide up Kili."

There are six official routes up Kilimanjaro. The most popular—and easiest—one is the Marangu route, or so-called tourist route. It's a well-marked, six-day trek with a string of huts along the way. The other routes range in difficulty from nontechnical mountaineering to technical rock and ice climbing. These less-traveled routes require guides and gear. Gear ranges from gaiters—rugged foot-to-knee leggings that keep pebbles, snow, and thorns out of your pants and shoes—to ice axes for climbing up walls of glacial ice.

I'd chosen to do the Shira route, a high-altitude nontechnical climb on the distant northwest side of the mountain. It led across the Shira Plateau, through the boulder-filled Western Breech, and into the northern ice fields of Kibo, the tallest of Kilimanjaro's two summits. (The second is a craggy 16,893 peak called Mawenzi.)

The nontechnical route required no rope. But getting to the top of Kibo required boulder scrambling, or climbing up rocks or cliffs by hand. It also required walking across fields of snow and ice. The push to the very tip top of Kibo—Uhuru Point—involved some exposure. That meant crossing some steep areas with little protection and sharp drop-offs, kind of like balancing on the edge of a bridge. Even more threatening would be the altitude, which plays deadly tricks with body and mind. Although I had handled altitude well in the past, nobody is ever safe from altitude sickness. It can strike even the most hardened climber.

Before setting out for the mountain, we had to sort out gear. When you climb, you pack and repack gear endlessly. You stare at piles on the floor and ask: "Do I have everything I need?" "Have I packed too much?" "Is there enough room for water?" "If not, what can I take out?"

The gear sorting took place at the white-washed Aishi Hotel. We dumped out our bags, and Wesley inventoried everything. All cotton came out. It took too long to dry. So did "luxury" items, such as extra changes of underwear or thermals. "Ounces count," said Wesley, "especially when you barely have enough oxygen to pull your own weight." "What about the porters?" a climber asked.

"They have to struggle with the food and cooking equipment," explained Wesley. "Besides," he added. "They leave us at 18,000 feet. If you make it that far, you go over the top of Kibo on your own."

Nothing came out of my pack. But something went in. "What are you going to do when your water and contact lenses freeze?" asked Wesley.

"What?" I replied.

"You have no insulated protectors," he said. "Once we hit 16,000 feet, you'll have to carry the bottles and lenses next to your body. You'll have to sleep with them, too."

Bill jumped in. "Don't worry, Wes. I brought extra. She'll take two of mine." Bill winked at me. "We're going to be climbing partners, I think."

I needed a climbing partner. Just like my partners on Mount Kackar, everybody on the Kili climb had more experience than me. They had either mountaineered, done rock climbing, or both. But I had trained, nearly every day. To prepare for the Kili climb, I did sixty-minute stints on the stair machine and bicycled hills in fourth gear. I even turned my yard into a gym.

My house perches on a near vertical slope that drops sharply to a stream. I used railroad ties to build terraces down the slope. Then, with headphones blaring rock 'n' roll, I climbed up and down those terraces hundreds of times with a 30-40 pound backpack. (ZZ Top works good on terraces. So does U2, The The, R.E.M. and Concrete Blond.) I sweated. But, at sea level, I had lots of oxygen to breathe. I could only hope that I'd handle the altitude well enough to carry 30 pounds over the summit on Kili. Nepal had taught me that I had a shot. And that's all I asked—a reasonable shot at the top.

After spending the night at the hotel, we headed to the dense equatorial forest at the edge of Kilimanjaro National Park. Wesley registered us. Then we drove up a deeply rutted road to meet our Chagga porters.

When we arrived at the start of the trail, a combination of fog and dense vegetation had cast a greenish twilight on the morning. A canopy of enmeshed tree branches sprawled overhead. Several kinds of sage, some more than 9 feet tall, grew on the ground. Ferns, lichens, and mosses mixed in with the sage. I still remember the musty smell and damp air. I strapped gaiters around my legs to protect them from scratches. I also dragged my rain gear from my pack. "Deb," called out Wesley. "Don't put on too many clothes. It's like a steam bath in the forest."

Before I could answer, my eyes fixed on a rifle carried by one of the porters. Wesley caught my gaze. "It's required by the park. More than monkeys and birds live in the forest. You don't want to mess around with an angry Cape

Buffalo or rogue elephant." I caught my breath. I hadn't thought about the animals.

"Wow! How many will we see?" I asked.

"None, I hope," grinned Wesley.

We plunged into the forest. Only a handful of people took this route each year. Overgrowth had covered parts of the trail. Torrential rains had washed out other parts. Here and there, twisted roots jutted up out of the ground. So much green and brown made the scattered pale pink orchids and purple violets seem brilliant in color.

To my delight, the forest also talked. Monkeys chattered. Birds sung, squealed, or whistled. And a distant elephant trumpeted. Overhead, Sykes monkeys with flowing black-and-white tails soared through the branches. As a brilliant red and black turaco flew overhead, it dropped a feather at my feet. I put it in my hat along with an orchid.

After traveling about two hours, I spotted a rare clearing in the forest. The rays of sun felt so good, I put down my pack and stripped off my poncho. Within seconds, I felt stinging all over my body. I let out a cry of pain. "*Siafu! Siafu!*" yelled one of the porters.

"What the hell are c-aa-foo?" I screamed.

"Army ants," answered Wesley. "You're covered with army ants."

Wesley ran over along with one of the porters. They began picking the ants off. "This is useless," said Wesley. "Forget the modesty. Get off some of those clothes." Nobody needed to convince me. I took off the top layers and gratefully got pelted with sand. I noticed one of the

climbers doubled over in laugher. My revenge came later that night. Some *siafu* got in his tent. Buff naked, he ran out for help. "How do you like the *siafu*?" I joked.

The first night on Kili brought lots of surprises for everyone. The porters kept a fire going to keep animals out of the camp. "Secure your water and food," directed Wesley. "Or you'll have visitors in your tent."

I joked, "No snakes, I hope."

He replied, "No, only *chatu*—pythons." A chill passed over me.

"I don't like pythons," I answered.

"Then take your light if you have to use a latrine," advised Wesley. "The night has eyes." I knew who the eyes belonged to—all the animals that hunted at night and slept during the day.

I cursed myself for drinking so much tea. I warned my bladder: "You'd better hold for eight hours. I don't want my butt nipped." But it ignored me. I closed my eyes and made a wish. Let all of that howling be bush babies—one-pound, big-eyed, tree-dwelling mammals with huge voices. I wrapped myself in Kangas—colorful Tanzanian cloth. Then I unzipped the tent and edged out into the dark. That midnight walk to the latrine sent my adrenaline rushing higher than any climb.

When I crawled back in my sleeping bag, I thought: In a few days, I'll be standing above the clouds. My feet will be planted on one of the rarest natural wonders on earth— tropical ice. Safe inside my tent, the howls of the bush babies turned into a lullaby. Soon I drifted off to sleep.

Going for the Top

Sometime around sunrise, an eerie silence settles on the equatorial forest. The animals that prowl the night go to sleep, and the animals that feed during the day wake up. The stillness woke me. I fumbled in the dark for my head-lamp and adjusted the light so that I could write in my journal.

When I climb big mountains, my journal is my closest friend and traveling companion. I tell it all the latest gossip. I also let it know my most private thoughts. I wrote until the sounds of Swahili let me know that the porters had gotten up to make breakfast. "Well, we're off again," I told my journal. "See you tonight."

After breakfast, we packed quickly. We had to cover a lot of ground. In a single day, we gained about 2,500 feet in altitude and passed through two ecological zones. The changes in plant and animal life were dazzling. The equatorial forest gave way to giant heather, trees of up to 40 feet. Here strands of lichen, known as "old man's beard," hung off branches like gray-green veils. Next came the moorlands, boglike terrain with smaller, bushier heather.

Around 11,000 feet, disaster hit. A wave of nausea spread over me. I vomited up breakfast, lunch, and anything else my stomach could pitch out. Wesley ran over.

"Whew! No blood. Can you keep moving?"

I felt lousy. But I had clear vision and no headaches. "Yea," I replied. "I can move."

He smiled. "You know, we don't always feel good at altitude. Part of the climb is pushing through it."

I asked the dreaded question: "Do you think it's altitude sickness?"

"I don't know," answered Wesley. "We'll see. Keep putting down water. You can't dehydrate."

Kili was the only time I've ever been sick on a mountain. But it terrified me. I had handled altitude so well. It was my ace. I played it whenever anybody questioned my ability to climb. "The altitude doesn't stop me," I'd explain. "It's a gift, and I plan to use it." I hoped that the nausea had come from moving too fast and eating too much food at lunch. I was so hungry that I had eaten some wild combinations—sardines, cheese, and eggs on roll slathered with mustard, followed by hot chocolate, a bunch of apricots, and a candy bar.

We camped at about 11,300 feet. The Shira Plateau, gateway to the Western Breech, lay ahead. I felt miserable. Wesley brought soup to my tent. Bill lent me a book. "Read," he directed. "Get your mind off the nausea."

After they left, I cried. "Don't let me go down so soon," I sobbed. "Let me at least break my old limit. Let me crack 18,200 feet."

I crawled into my sleeping bag and fell asleep. I don't remember moving all night. What I remember is the sound of my growling stomach. It made so much noise it woke me up. Daylight had barely broken. I ran into the porters' tent and blurted out: *"Kuna chakula gani?"* ("What is there to eat?") A porter named Abel (pronounced ab–BELL), smiled broadly: *"Mama. Pole! Pole!* (Mama. Slowly! Slowly!) We have anything you want."

Wesley stuck his head inside the tent. "I take it you're feeling better."

I reeled off, "You know it! I'm *sawa sawa!* I'm all right!"

Wesley crouched down beside me, "Let's keep you sawa sawa. I want you to start taking 250 milligrams of Diamox. You'll urinate a lot. But all the urination will keep the carbon dioxide out of your system. We can't risk edema."

My doctors had suggested that I carry Diamox. By reducing carbon dioxide levels, the Diamox would help prevent swelling of the brain (cerebral edema) and swelling of the heart (pulmonary edema). Edema is the biggest killer on the mountains. There's only one sure antidote—descent. And I didn't want to descend.

I already had peripheral edema—a swelling of the face, arms, and legs. My wrists and ankles were so puffy I hardly recognized them. Although this type of edema is relatively harmless, I didn't want to take any risks. So reluctantly I agreed to start the Diamox. Although a lot of climbers take Diamox, I still wonder whether my nausea had been caused by "pigging out" on the trail. Today I eat smaller meals, more often, with steady snacking.

As I swallowed the Diamox, Wesley said: "You've really got to drink water now. Dehydration will get you almost as quickly as the edema. I want to see you put down at least four quarts. Your urine should stay clear. If it gets cloudy, tell me. It means increased carbon dioxide—and trouble."

At breakfast, two other climbers, including Bill, showed up ill. "Altitude respects nobody," sighed Bill as he dropped down next to me. "I'm starting Diamox, too. You and I can compete for the latrines."

"It's a short, easy day," announced Wes over breakfast. "We'll head onto the Shira Plateau and camp at 12,300 feet. We should arrive by early afternoon. Enjoy the break. It's our last warm day. It's also our last shot at stream water. After this, we melt snow."

Both the air and the plants thinned as we headed upward. The amount of scree—loose volcanic pebbles—increased. Scree refuses to stay put. Imagine walking uphill on marbles. That's what scree can feel like. For every step forward, you feel like you're taking two steps backward. By the time I reached the Shira Plateau, my legs throbbed.

The afternoon passed peacefully on the plateau. Around 6:00 P.M., the clouds parted, revealing Kibo Peak. The setting sun put on a show, turning the peak shades of gold, red, and finally lavender. I decided to start talking to the mountain. *"Lala salama, Kibo. Tutaonana punde."* (Sleep peacefully, Kibo. We'll see each other soon.")

The next day, the push began. We trekked nearly eight hours across the Alpine zone—an area filled with shallow rooted plants and scattered tufts of dried grass. We trudged over miles of packed volcanic gravel peppered with football-sized rocks. Each step brought us closer to the dark lava cliffs of the Western Breech.

We set up camp at Lava Tower, a giant volcanic plug that once filled a huge lava funnel. A sea of fog and mist engulfed the camp by late afternoon.

I woke up feeling cold and damp. We only needed to ascend some 1,500 feet to get to the next camp. But it involved steep scree and fast-dropping temperatures. I didn't have much of an appetite, but I ate nonetheless. At altitude, breathing and walking consumes incredible calories. You sweat when climbing and shiver when resting. I've learned to more than double my food intake at altitude, yet I still lose weight!

Six hours of uphill ascent brought us to the edge of Arrow Glacier. My toes felt frostbitten. "Kick your boots against a rock," suggested Wesley. "That will get the blood moving."

I looked around at the campsite. "Home sweet home," I muttered. Fog, ice, and boulders. What more could a tired climber want?

I would have welcomed some rest. But we needed to acclimatize, or adjust, to the altitude gain expected on the next day's climb. For practice, we trudged up some 800

feet of scree. At about 16,100 feet, we used our feet to create mini-landslides and then rode the scree back into
camp. The "screeing" left me dusty and exhilarated. I'd
never skied pebbles before.

During the night, a small miracle happened. It snowed.
A five-inch white carpet covered the steep scree field. By
snow walking, we could save time and energy. But ultraviolet rays bounce more easily off snow. To prevent sun-
burn and damage to my eyes, I put on extra sunblock and
special ultraviolet sunglasses. The glasses even have side
flaps to prevent the rays from creeping in. With little oxygen to filter the rays, eye damage at altitude is a real threat.

Once on the snow, I used the walking mediation that
R.P. Lama had taught me in Nepal. Step, breathe out. Step,
breathe in. Step, breathe out. Step, breathe in. So it went
for hours. The repetition lulled me into a dreamlike calm-
ness. Every now and then, Wesley or Bill asked me to say
a sentence. They wanted to make sure the altitude had not
robbed me of my sanity. But I never felt more sane. This is
where I belonged—on the snow and ice.

By early afternoon, we reached 18,300 feet. Across a
broad plateau, I saw a huge gaping hole—the Inner
Crater. I smelled sulfur leaking out from fumaroles, or
smoke holes, in the crater floor. To the right, just beyond
the crater, sprawled huge glaciers. The glaciers stood several stories high. Yet they looked tiny against the huge
black wall of rock that rose to Uhuru Point—the highest
point in Africa. Uhuru is Swahili for "freedom." I thought,
How wonderful that the goal of my first big ascent should

be named after the gift given to me time and again by the mountains. Freedom, that's just what I feel when I climb.

I left the crater rim and headed into the snowfields. I dropped my pack, laid down in the snow, and started sweeping my arms back and forth. Abel, my Chagga porter, scrambled over.

"Mama, what are you doing?" he asked.

"Making snow angels," I answered.

"Why?" he wondered aloud.

"I told a little girl that angels lived on this mountain." I replied, "And I'm making sure a few do."

As I stared at the sky, I surrendered to the uniqueness of the moment. I wanted to stay here forever. But a swishing sound broke the spell. I looked over and saw Abel making snow angels. "What are *you* doing?" I laughed. "Making sure the little girl has lots of angels to see," replied Abel.

Partners in fantasy, Abel and I linked arms and walked back into camp. "What were you two doing?" asked one of the climbers.

"It's a secret," I responded. "I won't tell." Abel winked.

We camped next to the glaciers. When the sun set, temperatures plummeted below zero. Wesley handed me a candy bar. "Eat it if you get cold," he said. "It will force your body metabolism to act like a heater." He then gave me a warning. "I'm going to check you during the night. People breathe more slowly when they sleep. Pulmonary edema could set in. If you have trouble breathing, I'm sending you down with the porters. That goes for anyone else, too."

I crawled into my sleeping bag, along with water bottles, boots, and anything else I needed to keep warm. I keep sipping water to offset the Diamox. I cursed when I needed to urinate. But the curse faded into a blessing when I unzipped the tent. The moon hung over Kibo in a star-filled night. As wind whipped across the plateau, I realized that within hours I'd reach for the top of Africa. Maybe angels lived here after all.

Sunrise and a quick breakfast kicked off the final ascent. As I moved over the boulders and ice, I tried to control my breathing. I followed Bill. But he had a longer reach than me. On one scramble, I felt the exposure. Perched on a rock, I saw immense stretches of space all around me. I reached for a ledge on the next level and hauled myself up. This "power move" cost my breath. I thought oxygen would never return to my lungs. Bill saw my panic and walked to my side. "Take it easy," he said. "The air will come. Just don't try to suck it in all at once."

My breath returned. My heart stopped pounding. And I started climbing. Step by step, the summit came nearer. At the top, I saw a Tanzanian guide named Remi, one of Wesley's friends. Remi reached his hand to me as I cleared the last scramble. He pulled me up and hugged me. "Mama, you made it!" declared Remi.

I stood above the clouds. Ice and black obsidian crystals sparkled at my feet. I reached down to pick up a crystal to replace Charity's amethyst. "You collect rocks," guessed Bill.

"No," I replied, "I collect magic." He leaned over and

started picking up obsidian. "I think I'll start collecting some magic, too," he said softly. "In fact, let's take some extra magic home for our friends who need it."

Then, with the rest of the Shira climbers, Bill and I made our way over to the opposite side of the summit. We looked down on the huge scree bank that marked the top of the so-called tourist route. An easy descent faced us. One by one, we shuffled our feet and started screeing our way off the mountain.

Seven little dust clouds greeted a single climber huffing and puffing his way up the tourist route. "Where did you guys come from?" he yelled.

"Through the Western Breech," I responded.

"Tough route!" he answered. "Was it a good climb?"

"The best!" I laughed.

As I screed away, I wondered: What made this climb *the best*? Would the tourist route have been just as good? Would another route have been even better? A summit is a summit, isn't it? So what made the climbs different? An answer came to me in a flash. The journey—that's what makes a climb special. If my goal was to "bag peaks," I'd just try to get to the top as quickly and easily as possible. No, I thought, I'm a journeyer. The magic lies in the route chosen. The greater the challenge, the higher the risks, the more chances for surprises. I thought about people who asked if mountain climbing was risky. "Yes," I thought out loud. "It sure is. I risk having the time of my life."

Heading Out Alone

Pieces of thread dangled from my toes. "The thread will allow the blisters to drain," said Wesley as he ran a needle and thread through four huge blisters. He looked at my black-and-blue toenails as he sewed. "You'll probably lose all ten," he added, "Remember how much you swell at altitude. Buy even bigger boots for your next climb. Wear double socks until your feet swell to fit the boots."

The descent off Kilimanjaro had hurt my feet. With each step, my bloated feet jammed forward in my boots until they throbbed with pain. Yet, as I hobbled to a celebration dinner with the rest of the climbers, I took a kind of pride in my feet. "Yea, I climbed a mountain," boasted my right foot. "Yea, I did, too," boasted the left.

I hardly recognized everybody without their mountain grime and gear. Surveying my dress, Bill asked, "Do I know you?" Then he looked down at my rubber thongs, "Oh, yes, I know those feet. You must be Deborah."

Seated around the table, we talked about food. "I think I'll have sardines, peanut butter, and packaged soup," joked one climber. That, of course, is standard climbing fare. What we all really wanted was peppery Tanzanian stews and steamed vegetables.

As we waited for our food, each of us received an award. "We got to know each of you pretty well," said a guide named Lee. "So tonight we're honoring your 'special talents.'"

Lee handed out award after award: Golden Heart Award, Surreptitious Scientist Award, Bonso Man Award, and more. Finally, my turn came. Lee announced: "While the rest of us sat glued to our cameras and binoculars, she serenely soaked up the soul of Tanzania. For her single-minded effort to commit East Africa to memory, we award Deborah the Sensory Intake Award." I erupted in laughter as Lee pinned on my medal—an acacia leaf and thorn.

"Did you take any pictures at all?" asked one of the climbing shutterbugs. "A few," I responded. Then several people threw back words I had used a dozen times on the mountain. "No picture will equal the memories."

On Kilimanjaro, I meditated whenever I could, just as I do on most climbs. The meditation follows a pattern. I close my eyes and focus on the smells. After savoring the odors, I let in the sounds, one by one, until they build into a natural harmony. Then I feel the weather play across my body—the heat or cold, the dew or frost, the dust or mist. Finally, I slowly open my eyes. "Look at the colors first," I tell my mind's eye. "Now look at the shapes. Let the images come last."

Each time a vision appears—a tree, an animal, a distant ridge or peak—its intensity startles me. No experience can rival it. No human-made substance—alcohol or drugs—can ever make you feel higher. If I have an addiction, it's to these mountain meditations, to the memories of the journey.

Not all memories involve mountains. Many are people-filled. I recall the guides or teachers who make the journeys possible. I remember the climbers who share the trails or the trekking huts. I think of the nonclimbers who enrich my trips or teach me lessons when I head out alone.

After climbing Kilimanjaro, I set out on my own to explore East Africa. During my travels, I came in contact with people who changed the direction of future journeys. I had promised the immigration official in Moshi, Tanzania, to donate my medical kit. I chose to leave it at a clinic overrun with refugees in Mombassa, Kenya.

I spotted the clinic while walking through the streets of Mombassa. People of all ages sat outside in the street. "*Unatoka wapi?*" I asked. ("Where are you coming from?") "Somalia," replied one weary voice. The single-word answer said it all. Civil war and famine had devastated Somalia.

"*Tafadhali hodi,*" I murmured as I edged my way into the clinic. ("Please let me pass.")

Once inside, I found a nurse who could speak English. She accepted my medical kit, but with a qualification. "We cannot handle the refugees," said the nurse. "Some of our own people, such as the Turkana in northern Kenya, face starvation. We have too little money and too few hands."

Looking at the line of people waiting for treatment, I asked: "Will two more hands be of any help? If so, you can put mine to work."

I spent two days at the clinic. It was not a lot of time. Nor did I work with the Somalian refugees who suffered the most. Most of these refugees died of starvation and disease. But the experience led me to make a promise: "Every time I climb overseas," I vowed, "I will try to do service in the region I visit." I wanted to share, in a very small way, the good fortune that allows me to climb in far-away mountains.

In 1993, the lure of the mountains pulled my heart and soul back to the Himalayas. The journey began with a telephone call to a friend named Heidi. "Didn't you work in a mission in India?" I asked.

"Wow! I sure did," Heidi replied. "One day I wandered into an orphanage in Old Delhi, and I ended up staying for more than three months. What do you want to know about it?"

"Everything," I responded, "right down to the directions on how to get there."

I listened as Heidi talked. "Mother Teresa founded the mission. It's filled with children, especially infants. Women too poor to raise more children come there to deliver their babies. You can't take pictures, Deb. The sisters at the mission follow Mother Teresa's vow: 'No recognition for spiritual work on earth.' I'll give you directions any rickshaw driver can follow. When you get to the mission, ask for Sister Tina. Tell her Heidi said 'hello.'"

Heidi's experiences at the mission and in the rest of India, helped me form my plans. After working at the mission, I'd travel down the Ganges to Varanasi, the most sacred of all Hindu cities. Just outside of Varanasi lay Sarnath. Here Siddhartha Gautama, the Buddha, preached his four nobel truths—the principles that form the basis of Buddhism. I'd meditate where the Buddha and countless other pilgrims had meditated before me.

After spending time at these two spiritual centers, I'd travel by railroad and car or bus into Sikkim—the home of Kanchenjunga, the third highest mountain in the world. Even fewer people have climbed Kanchenjunga than Everest. So I knew I'd never scale the mountain's icy walls. But I'd get as close as possible.

I arrived in Delhi, the capital of India, in late August 1993. The city lay at the northwestern edge of the Himalayan foothills. Like many ancient cities, history pulls Delhi in two directions. New Delhi, with its modern buildings, looks to the present. Old Delhi, with its red sandstone forts and palaces, looks to the past.

Most of Delhi's poor live in the rundown buildings near the forts and palaces. Here Mother Teresa built her mission. I found no shortage of work at the mission. I changed diapers, washed bottles, and rocked babies. Caring for a dormitory full of infants is a lot more exhausting than climbing a mountain. Once, while folding clean diapers, I fell asleep in a huge laundry pile on the floor.

One of the sisters shook me awake and handed me a baby. Feeding time had started all over again.

While working at the mission, I met other volunteers, including some from the United States. They helped me figure out how to get into Sikkim. "You'll need to make railroad connections," said a volunteer named Anne. "But be prepared to forget your feminism. You'll have to stand in the women's ticket line. There's only one line for women and more than ten for men. So wait an hour or hire a man to buy a ticket for you."

I chose to stand in line. Nearly ninety minutes later, I reached the ticket window. I told the agent, "I want to book tickets from Delhi to Varanasi and from Varanasi to Siliguri (a station near the edge of Sikkim)."

"Madam," he replied, "I can sell you a ticket only as far as Varanasi. From there, you must figure out the rest of your journey."

Startled, I asked, "Can I get to Siliguri?"

"Perhaps, if the train is not full," he said. "Or perhaps you'll travel to Calcutta and try to book a train from there."

"More women's lines," I moaned.

I assumed that somehow, someway, I'd get to Siliguri. But I still needed a permit to get into Sikkim. As a former independent kingdom, Sikkim had kept certain rights when it joined India in 1975. These rights included regulation of tourism. So I headed to the Sikkim Tourist Office.

At the office, I met a young Sikkimese official named Tej Pal. "Why do you want to go to Sikkim?" asked Tej Pal.

"I want to get as close to Kanchenjunga as possible, perhaps even climb some of it." I replied. "Can you help me?"

Tej Pal smiled, "I can only give you a permit. But to visit the mountain, you must see a very important friend of mine in Gangtok. His name is Y. Dorjee (E. Doo ZGEE). Call this number and tell him your dream." I copied down the number, not knowing how important Dorjee and his family would soon become to me.

With ticket and permit in hand, I said good-bye to the mission. That night, I boarded a train and chugged nearly fourteen hours across India. With rain falling, I arrived in Varanasi, the oldest city in the world.

Most Hindus hope to visit Varanasi at least once in their lives. According to sacred Hindu writings known as the Upanishads, Varanasi is the eternal resting place of Shiva, one of the most important Hindu gods. Each year, thousands of Hindus come to Varanasi to honor Shiva and bathe in the sacred Ganges River. In life, Hindus seek the water for relief of sins. In death, they seek cremation on a pile of sandalwood along the water's edge. In this way, a Hindu's ashes can mingle with *Ma Ganges* (Mother Ganges), the giver of life.

As I walked from the train station to find a room, pilgrims filled the street. Sitar music drifted from dozens of temples. Street vendors sold "leaf boats" to float on the river. Incense hung heavy in the air. Like many of the visitors, I planned to bathe in the Ganges.

The next morning, at sunrise, I made my way to the river. People sang or murmured songs related to the

Ganges. As my ears adjusted to the sound, I heard an often-repeated chant: *"Ganga Maiya Ki Jay"* ("Glory for the Mother Ganga.") With a Tanzanian Kanga cloth wrapped tightly around me, I walked into the river. I tried not to make eye contact. But people touched me and smiled. I set a leaf boat adrift and said a meditation: "Lead me to the source of Ma Ganga. Guide me into the Himalayas."

Meditation filled the days in Varanasi and Sarnath. Then the time came to tackle the train station once again. It took arguing, bartering, bribing, and lots of patience to get a ticket to Siliguri. Rupees, or Indian dollars, passed hands several times before an agent met me behind the train station with a ticket. Before running off, he said, "Give the conductor some rupees to guard you in the night." As I pushed my way into an overnight sleeper packed with men, I felt the rupees would be well spent. I probably would have been safe. But as a single woman traveling alone, I would rest more peacefully under the conductor's watchful eye.

As the train clattered over the tracks, I pulled a thin cotton curtain around my narrow berth. By dawn, I would have traveled more than halfway across the subcontinent of India. I had no precise route in mind for the days to come. Any route would be okay so long as it headed to Kanchenjunga. Before drifting off to sleep I thought, The adventure lies in the journey.

9

On the Wings of Angels

The train pulled into Siliguri with the dawn. Kanchenjunga, here I come, I thought as I scrambled onto the platform. My eyes searched around for clues on how to get into Sikkim. My eyes fixed on a clump of travelers. (Their backpacks gave them away.) I walked over to see if they, too, were headed into Sikkim.

I've learned that a backpack can be a passport into the mountains from almost any country in the world. So when I plunged into the group, I asked, "Any of you guys speak English?"

A booming voice answered, "Where do you come from?"

I replied, "The United States of America" "Hello American," responded the voice. "I am from Russia. You have heard that there is no more Soviet Union. We are free to travel now. I am Vladimir. This is my wife Alexis. Like you, we want to see the world. I think maybe we'll have a lot to talk about."

Other English-speaking travelers joined the conversation. We compared notes on how to get into Gangtok, the capital of Sikkim. "Buses cost less," said one person. "But taxis travel faster with fewer breakdowns," said another.

We also discussed the weather. "Are the monsoons over?" asked a hiker from New Zealand. "I don't want to run into any mud slides at this elevation." We all weighed the question carefully.

"It's early September," I responded. "The monsoons should have passed by now."

A Sikkimese taxi driver jumped into the conversation. "We're cleaning up the mud slides now. I know all the open routes. I can give you a good price."

A woman that I'll call Pat (not her real name) grabbed onto me. She said, "Let's take the cab. I can't stand the thought of being packed onto a bus."

Vladimir overheard Pat. "Alexis and I will come, too," he called out. "We'll split the cost."

Pat ignored Vladimir and negotiated a price for two riders. "Come on," she said to me. "Let's get out of here."

Before I could say "no," the cab driver rushed off with my backpack. I pushed into the seat next to Pat and asked, "Why did you do that?"

"India's got too many people already." she replied, "I don't need to have my cab full of people, too."

I cringed. My instincts screamed, "Watch out! This woman is trouble." My conscience said, "Don't be so quick to judge." I should have listened to my instincts.

As the cab headed up twisting roads, the driver asked:

"Do you know what Sikkim means?" Without waiting for an answer, he continued. "It comes from the Sanskrit word *Shikhim*, meaning 'crested.' In all of Sikkim, you will not find a single kilometer of flat land. It's all mountains."

"I love mountains," mused Pat. She then rattled off a list of summits that she'd climbed. "Peak bagger," I grumbled to myself. "Jealous?" asked my conscience.

When we pulled into Sikkim, the cab driver dropped us off at a hotel. A room cost about $30 a night—expensive for Sikkim, but a bargain for me.

As soon as possible, I called E. Dorjee, a respected business owner whose family included a long line of Buddhist leaders. When I asked to see Kanchenjunga, Dorjee replied: "I'm sorry. It's not climbing season yet. Even if it was, we need four packs, or four climbers, to get a permit. On a clear morning, when the clouds part, you can see the summit from your hotel."

My voice cracked as I spoke, "I've traveled so far and with so much hope. Is there really no way to get me to the base camp?"

After a moment of silence, Dorjee said, "I'll see what I can do. Can you find someone to travel with you? It will help me get a permit."

Pat immediately sprang to mind. I thought: How can a climber turn down 28,150 feet of mountain? Her answer surprised me. "Only if there are porters," she said. "I don't carry weight on my back."

Startled, I asked, "How did you climb all those peaks?"

Without blinking, she answered: "I hired someone to

carry my gear. Or I traveled with a boyfriend. You can carry weight, if you want. I don't do it."

I wanted to say "Forget it!" But I wanted the permit more. Besides we were only going to 15,800 feet. I could use the low altitude to train for future climbs. I needed—and wanted—the experience of climbing under weight. Without it, I'd never make a "committed climb," one that requires climbing a mountain with a single partner. So I said, "I'll see if we can get a porter for you. I'll carry my own gear and some of the food."

Dorjee made the trip happen. He increased the number of packs by sending along his 16-year-old daughter Dolma and a foster son named Pasang. We now had the required four climbers, plus a porter. Pasang, who came from a mountain village in western Sikkim, knew the route to the base camp. He'd serve as a guide.

Dorjee drove us to the trekking hut at the start of the trail. As we traveled over rugged roads, he talked about the mountain. "Nobody reached the top of Kanchenjunga until 1975," he said. "Many climbers believe it's a harder mountain than Everest. Those who first climbed it stopped short of the summit. They knew that the Sikkimese considered it sacred. So they didn't stand on the summit until Sikkim gave its permission."

I liked the story. The climbers risked their lives knowing they'd never reach the summit. But they claimed something special nonetheless—the challenge of a first ascent, the pioneering of the first route up a mountain. They definitely were journeyers. They just headed in the direction they loved best—up.

When Dorjee dropped us at the end of the trail, he went over the map one more time. As we set out, he shouted: "Say hello to Kanchenjunga. Ask its spirit to protect Sikkim—and all of you." Then with a wave of his hand, Dorjee said: "See you in five days."

I barely saw or spoke to Pat as she sprinted ahead on the trail. With 45 pounds on my back, I moved much slower. Plus, I loved the journey. If I went too fast, I might miss something along the trail.

Dolma and I had lots of time to talk. We shared stories about growing up. "At what age did you become a woman?" asked Dolma. "When did you fall in love?" We threw questions back and forth for hours. Then, in a cautious voice, Dolma asked, "Deborah, do you believe in angels?"

The question stunned me. I replied, "My friend Charity says that people who believe in angels always manage to meet each other."

"Does that mean yes?" demanded Dolma.

I hugged her and responded, "Yes, it means yes."

Dolma and I now compared Christian and Buddhist angels. We decided that angels were angels, regardless of their religion. We talked so intently that neither of us noticed the narrowing trail. Instead, we absentmindedly pushed plants out of the way with our feet.

After a while, my feet began to itch. Then they stung. When I looked down, I saw blood oozing from my boots. As Dolma gazed at her own blood-soaked socks, she yelled, *"Juggas!* Our shoes are filled with juggas."

When we pulled off our boots, I met my first juggas— the leeches that come with the monsoons. In the wet weather, they grow on plants almost like fine hair. When people brush against them, the leeches attach themselves and suck blood until they swell into the size of stubby worms. The monsoons may have just ended, but the juggas had not.

Pasang heard the commotion and came running back. He pulled a can of kerosene from his pack and wet a rag. "Use this to wipe off the juggas," ordered Pasang. "Only kerosene or salt will knock them off." He then said, "Walk single file and don't touch the plants. We'll leave the wet zone soon."

Soon meant six hours, an overgrown trail, and more juggas. Even Pat did not move fast enough to miss the juggas. But without weight she could reach the first trekking hut more quickly.

As I slogged along the trail, I learned to welcome the sight of a suspension bridge across a river or stream. Free of plants, the bridges gave me a chance to pull off a few more juggas. When the juggas finally disappeared, I faced the cold temperatures of higher altitude. Cold, tired, and blood-covered, I made my way to the trekking hut.

"You sure travel slow," said Pat. "You'd better pick up your speed if you ever want to climb glaciers. You don't want to get stuck on steep-angled ice in the dark."

As I dropped my 45-pound pack on the floor, I nearly exploded. But I had to spend at least four more days with

Pat. So with a controlled voice I answered, "I pace myself. I've climbed up to fifteen hours without stopping. I hear endurance counts."

After supper, I dropped onto a cot in a room shared with Dolma. "Why do I climb?" I asked her.

"Good question," replied Dolma. "When you figure out the answer, let me know." We started laughing and prayed for juggas to disappear from earth.

For the next two days, fog and cold drizzle made the journey to the base camp miserable. Once there, dense clouds blanketed the summit of Kanchenjunga. Buddhist prayer flags marked the start of trails leading to the high camps. But we'd go no farther. The mountain had chosen not to reveal itself.

In honor of the hidden peak, Pasang built a fire. As he repeated Buddhist prayers, he threw a cookie and a cup of tea into the flames. Pasang caught my gaze. "It's time to return," he said. "Perhaps on another trip, you will touch Kanchenjunga." He then signaled for us to begin our two-day descent.

With no hope of seeing Kanchenjunga, Pat wanted to get out of the mountains fast. "Can I get down in a day?" she asked Pasang.

"You saw the trails," he replied. "They're too narrow to risk darkness. We'll stay at a trekking hut." With these words, Pat sprinted ahead to the hut.

"Why does she go so fast?" I wondered aloud. "Do you think she's in a hurry to get to the juggas?" As Dolma laughed, I added, "I really don't understand why she climbs."

When I went to bed that night, I felt the journey had almost ended. I never guessed that the next day would bring me face-to-face with death. Instead, I went to sleep dreaming of hot showers and clean clothes.

The morning revealed another gray, damp day. "Go slowly," advised Pasang. "The trail is slippery." A slow pace suited me fine, especially when parts of the trail fell sharply by several hundred feet. As we traveled, the day got darker and the clouds thicker. Rain began to fall. As the drops got bigger and faster, Pasang muttered, "Monsoons. They haven't ended."

Pat had her own answer to the worsening situation. She shouted: "I'm going ahead to meet Dorjee."

When she reached into the porter's bag to grab a flashlight, I said sharply, "Pat, that leaves us with just one light."

She snapped, "Don't expect me to keep your pace, especially with all these leeches." "Three of us are carrying packs," I threw back. "If we go too fast, we risk falling. And if the batteries in my flashlight burn out, we're definitely in trouble."

With a toss of her head, she said, "See you in camp."

As I watched Pat sprint off without a pack, I felt keenly aware of the weight on my own shoulders. "It's not good to separate," said Pasang. He then took Dolma's pack and said: "Keep up with her. Tell Dorjee to send help if we're delayed for too long."

Dolma turned to me and asked, "Will you be all right?"

"Climb safely." I said, "We'll meet you later."

As I slogged through the mud, I felt the itch and sting of

juggas. I tried to pull leeches from my hands, face, and neck. But I could do nothing about the ones that wiggled their way into my shoes or up the legs of my pants. We had to keep moving before the trail washed out.

Mud can be more dangerous than ice. It's totally unpredictable. When a mud slide sent a spray of trees and boulders crashing onto the trail, we crossed the barricade on our hands and knees. It felt safer to crawl than to stand on a muddy, grease-like surface.

On the other side, Pasang asked, "Can you reach your flashlight?"

"Yes," I replied.

"Take it out," he continued. "It's getting too dark to walk safely."

A thin ray of light now guided our footsteps. Intent on looking for dangers ahead, I missed a slick patch of mud at my feet. A misplaced step suddenly sent me into a fall. In a split second, I realized that I was going over the edge of the trail.

Time seemed to stop. I listened to the stream crashing against rocks far below me. I studied the color of a moonless night. I felt the air flow over my body. Spinning in a freefall, three thoughts passed through my mind: I didn't say good-bye to everybody. I hope it doesn't hurt. And, with a wicked smile, my mother said this would happen.

Caught in a half laugh, I slammed into a small tree growing out of the steep-sided slope. As I reached around its trunk, I realized I still held the flashlight. Pasang had used the light to trace my fall. He yelled, "I'm coming down."

I shouted back, "Don't do it. There's no need for two of us to die."

Pasang's answer came in the form of deep-throated Buddhist chants.

He's coming, I thought. I quickly stuck the flashlight in my mouth to serve as a beacon. This left one hand free to grab Pasang. As the chants came nearer, I saw Pasang sailing down the mud bank on his belly. By a miracle, he, too, hit the tree. Together, we clawed our way up some 30 feet of slime.

Covered with mud and leeches, we started down the trail. On a suspension bridge, we ran into Pat. Dolma sat miserably by her side. "Her flashlight burned out," said Dolma. Panic-stricken by darkness and leeches, Pat screamed, "Get me out of here."

I almost choked with fury. I wanted to shake her and say: "You left us with one light and three packs. I almost died. Now you want my help!" Instead, I closed my eyes and calmed the inner storm within me. Two out-of-control people would not help the situation.

"I have the only flashlight," I said. "If you want to get out of this mess, link hands with us." We formed a human chain, with me in the lead. As I walked, I shined the light close to my feet. I shouted out warnings to the others. "Don't trip on the tree root." "Watch out for the mud pool." "Hill up ahead."

By the time we staggered to the trail's end, 18-leech filled hours had passed. Dorjee rushed to meet us. Worry etched his face. "Thank Lord Buddha," he said. "You're okay."

I spent the next hour salting juggas and washing off mud and blood. As I crawled in my sleeping bag, I felt an ache in my shoulder. I didn't realize yet that it had been dislocated by the fall. Instead, I thought it was just more of the many pains that racked my body.

Dorjee sat down beside me with a pot of tea. "Drink this," he said. "Tomorrow, when you've rested, I have something to show you."

The next day, the sun finally appeared. As we drove out of the mountains, rainbows arched in the clouds. Butterflies sailed around flowers. My fall seemed liked a dream. "Did it really happen?" I wondered. My aching shoulder replied, "Feel me. It happened."

Dorjee kept his destination a surprise. After traveling three hours, he pulled his truck into the Pemayangtse Monastery. "It's called the Perfect Sublime Lotus," explained Dorjee. "It's the heart of all the monasteries in Sikkim." Then, with a beaming face, he said, "My family helped found it."

Dorjee led me into the monastery and up a set of twisting stairs. At the top, he unlocked a heavy wooden door. As it swung open, I saw a huge painted carving. Dorjee began to speak softly. "My father had visions. He saw the entire world—not just the world of the living, but the world of the dead and the world of *bodhisattvas*. He made this carving to teach us about the visions. He worked single-handedly for five years. Look up, Deborah. What do you see?"

I raised my eyes and saw winged beings riding on rainbows. "They're the bodhisattvas," said Dorjee. "They have so much compassion that they chose to stay among the world of the living so that they can help us. Dolma told me you believe in angels. My father saw bodhisattvas, the Buddhist form of angels. So I know that angels exist. It was the bodhisattvas who guided you through the mountains. They have given you a spirit to fly—to live among the mountains."

Before leaving the monastery, Dorjee gave me a Tibetan prayer book. He helped me translate one of the prayers. To this day, I carry it with me on climbs. One line reads: "When parted from my beloved friends wandering alone, I fearlessly recognize myself."

The mountains don't just teach me about climbing. They teach me about me. Sometimes that can be the scariest part of a climb. After tackling mud slides in Sikkim, I felt ready to tackle the type of climbing that I feared the most—technical rock climbing. I wondered what I would learn about myself as I inched my way up cliffs or hung off ledges hundreds of feet above the ground. I hoped the angels were ready to catch me again.

On the Rocks

"Reach to your right. There's a handhold just above your head. If it's too high, move out on the rock face to your right so that you can stand on the flake—that wafer of rock—a couple of inches below your knee. You just have to push on it a second and you'll have that handhold. Come on, Deb, you can do it."

As Daniel spun off the directions, I went blank. My dyslexia kicked in big time. Too many directions, too fast. My brain went fuzzy as I tried to visualize right from left. I froze on the rock face.

"What's wrong?" asked Daniel. "You've done a lot harder climbs than this. Your body is too close to the rock. Put more of your weight over your feet. If you don't balance your weight, you're going to fall."

Suddenly, I exploded. "What do you think I am, some kind of ant? My hands and feet just don't stick to the rocks. You know I'm dyslexic. I can't tell right from left. I hate climbing."

"Let go of the rocks," said Daniel. "I'm going to lower you down." But I couldn't let go of the rocks either. A cold, clammy sweat began to soak my clothes. I felt dizzy. And then I fell.

Daniel—my friend, climbing teacher, and mountain soulmate—saw the fall coming. A rope connected us. As soon as my feet went off the rock, Daniel tightened his grip on the end of the rope with what is known as the brake hand. He then pulled his arm down until the rope got tight. I swung forward into the rock. But I only suffered two bruised knees and a scraped hand.

When my feet touched the ground, Daniel asked: "What happened up there?"

My mind raced for an answer. "It's the fall in Sikkim. I can't take heights anymore."

Daniel's voice softened. "Lots of us have fallen. We have to work through the fear. Remember, on the rocks you're tied into a rope. I won't let you get hurt. Except for a few bruises, what do you have to be afraid of?"

At this last question, I burst into tears. The fall in Sikkim had left me rattled. I had rock climbed on and off ever since Kilimanjaro. The height never bothered me. What did bother me was all the skill involved in rock climbing. Too many knots to tie, too many lefts and rights to figure out.

My first climbing teacher understood dyslexia. He said: "People with dyslexia learn more slowly. But once they learn something, they don't forget it. It just takes time for their brain to draw its own picture."

For me, it felt like it took forever. I spent months learning how to tie a figure eight—the basic knot for tying a climbing rope to a harness. I always had to ask for help. I had the same trouble mastering a new technique. I know today that when rock climbers fall, they try the route again and again until they figure out how to get past the crux, or hardest part of the climb. That's how they learn. But when I started climbing rocks, falling felt like failing.

I kept at the rocks for one simple reason. When I finally succeeded, I felt a freedom and joy beyond words. Once my climbing teacher said, "You looked like a ballerina on the rocks today." That compliment carried me through all the klutsy moves of the next month.

After my dislocated shoulder healed, I asked Daniel to take me on a safe rock climb. "Make it easy," I said. "It's my first time on the rocks in almost seven months." As I inched up higher and higher, memories of Sikkim kicked in, and I panicked. "What are you doing up this high?" I asked myself. "There's no such thing as a safe climb!"

The fear and confusion felt overwhelming. Trapped between the rock and my fear, I froze. When Daniel's voice interrupted my panic, yet another fear kicked in. "What made me put so much trust in another person?" I asked silently. The more directions Daniel gave, the more I wished he would vanish.

Rock climbing, like high-altitude ice climbing, makes you dependent upon a partner for your safety—and for your life. I didn't know if I wanted to be that dependent upon anyone. On the rocks, all your fears and hang-ups are often exposed. And suddenly I felt terrified at being so open to another person, especially a man. Standing on the ground in tears, I thought, You're an emotional chicken.

"Want to talk about it?" asked Daniel as he put his arm around my shoulders. Still sniffling, I made a decision. This lack of trust both in myself and in a partner was messing up my climbing—and probably my life. I blurted out, "I don't like anybody seeing me this scared. Maybe you won't want to climb with me. Even if you do, I don't know if I trust you or anybody else to hold me on a rope while I scramble a hundred feet off the ground. I can't promise you, me, or anybody I won't fall."

Daniel laughed. "How do you think I felt the first time you held me on a rope? I'm 6 feet 2 inches and 180 pounds. You think I didn't worry?"

Now I started laughing. "You surprised me by falling on our first climb," I recalled.

"That's right," said Daniel. "I knew I wouldn't fall far. So I tested your reaction to get rid of *my* fear."

Daniel and I worked out a plan for climbing. To get around my dyslexia, we imagined the rock as a giant clock. "Reach for 10 o'clock" made sense to me. I could see the picture of a clock in my mind. We'd also agreed to focus on basic rock climbing techniques until the moves felt comfortable again. Finally, I agreed to take risks—and even fall—if it meant I might learn a new skill.

At first, we stuck to top roping—a type of climbing in which the rope is hooked through an anchor at the top of a cliff. It takes a lot of hands-on experience to set up a top

rope. All the equipment—sturdy slings and oval alu-
minum alloy rings called carabiners—must be in the right
place and at the right angles. They also must be hooked to
an absolutely solid rock or tree. Your life depends on it!
Finally the rope needs to slip through the carabiners, or
"biners," just at the edge of the cliff. Nothing frays a rope
quicker than dragging it across the sharp edge of a rock.

Daniel put me on a top rope because it reduced risk.
With both ends of the rope hanging down from the
anchor, the top rope acts like a pulley. One end of the pulley ties into the harness of the climber. The other end slips
through a special device known as a belay plate attached
to the harness of the person who holds the rope. The rope
handler—known as the belayer—is hooked into another
anchor on the ground. If the climber falls, the belayer
won't be pulled off his or her feet.

The belayer does not pull a climber up the rocks. The
belayer feeds out extra rope, or slack, as the climber heads
up the rock. And if the climber falls, the belayer pulls the
rope tight to stop the fall. I can even stop Daniel, who
weighs nearly twice as much as me.

After I panicked on the rocks, I found it hard to even do
top roping. I'd tie the rope into my harness and start call-
ing out the basic voice commands used by climbers. "On
belay?" I'd ask. If Daniel had set up the belay, he'd answer,
"Belay on." I'd wait for him to pull in any extra slack until
I felt a gentle tug on my waist. Then I'd call out, "climbing." With a smile Daniel would respond, "Climb away."
But I could go just so far before I lost my nerve. "Watch

me," I'd yell. In climber's language, this meant "I think I'm going to fall."

Daniel tried to come up with solutions. He began by putting me on easier routes. A rating system first introduced by the Sierra Club categorizes climbs by the level of skill and equipment required. Class 1-3 climbs generally require no rope. Class 4 climbs may have enough exposure that an average climber may want a rope. A Class 5 climb almost always involves rope.

Within Class 5 climbs, the levels of difficulty vary greatly. So a group of climbers in Yosemite, California, added decimals to the climbs. The ratings range from 5.1 to 5.14. At 5.10 and after, letters from *a* to *d* are added. At higher levels, climbers may be scaling up small wrinkles or holding onto tiny fractures in the rocks. Or they may be swinging out on an overhang with nothing but open space beneath them. With a power move, they try to go over the top. Needless to say, correct placement of gear is a matter of life and death.

Before my fall in Sikkim, I climbed 5.6. But no matter how hard Daniel tried, he couldn't talk me back up to this level. So he dropped me back to 5.5, then 5.4, and finally 5.3. Still I froze at some point in the climb. Finally, Daniel tried another approach. "I'm going to climb like we used to," he said. "I'm going to lead up the rocks. When I'm at the top, you'll follow and take out all the gear. You'll be on your own. Think you're up to it?"

"What level are we going to climb?" I asked Daniel hesitantly. "Oh, I don't know. Maybe a 5.4." He then strapped his rack—a belt loaded with all kinds of metal climbing equipment—around his waist. He threw a few slings around one shoulder and the coiled rope around the other. As Daniel headed off to select a route, he casually said: "Did you bring your chalk bag? I seemed to remember that you liked to chalk up your hands when they sweated. You said it gave you time to mediate."

Daniel picked a route called "Tadpole." (Every established route has a name given to it by the person who pioneered it.) The route seemed to require three or four techniques. It started with a rock formation called a dihedral. The formation looked just like its nickname—open book. I'd have to stem the rock, or spread my feet on two walls that joined together in a deep V. A crack crept up the V, gradually getting wider and wider until it opened onto a ledge. The crack, I guessed, must be the tadpole.

I tried to visualize the climb. Somehow I'd have to find hand holds in the crack while I stemmed my feet up higher and higher. When the crack got wide enough, I'd jam my feet into it and try to edge up high enough to reach the ledge. Then I'd plant my hands on the ledge, press down on my palms, and lift myself up. This technique, known as "manteling," also allows me to "smear" with my feet.

Climbing shoes look like ballet slippers with a lot of rubber on the soles. "Smearing" allows you take advantage of the rubber. You press down on the front of your feet to gain friction and really walk up the rock like an ant.

My eyes fixed on the formation above the ledge. A small overhang jutted out. Somehow I had to get over it or around it to complete the climb. That's the crux, I thought. I'll freeze for sure.

Daniel seemed to read my mind. "I don't care how you climb it. Just get up any way you can."

"This is no 5.4," I shot back.

"Sure it is," said Daniel. "Your fear has robbed you of your perspective. Everything looks harder to you."

With these words, Daniel set up an anchor on a tree. "Get ready to go on belay," he directed. "You're going to hold me." We called out the climbing commands to each other. Then Daniel started heading up the rock. When he got to a difficult section, Daniel placed his first piece of gear—also known as a "nut' or "chock"—snugly in the crack. He then yanked on it. Satisfied that the nut would hold, Daniel clipped a carabiner through a metal loop at the end of it. He then clipped the rope through the carabiner. This was his first anchor. If Daniel fell, the anchor would break his fall—that is, if I snapped my brake hand in place.

I watched Daniel so intently that I forgot that I'd soon follow him. He placed gear every three feet or so. This would control his fall. Plus if one piece of gear popped out, there'd be another. When Daniel got to the top, he yelled down "Off belay!" That meant: "I'm secure. I no longer need your belay." I unhooked myself and yelled: "Belay off." To a climber this means: "You can pull up all the extra rope when you are ready."

I couldn't see Daniel. They only way we communicated was through these basic commands. As Daniel pulled up the slack, I held onto the end. I needed enough rope to tie a figure eight knot into my harness. When the rope went tight, I called out: "That's me." This command told Daniel the rope wasn't caught in a rock.

My thoughts raced as Daniel hooked up a new belay at the top of the cliff. I wondered, "How on earth will I clean the rock, or take out all the gear?" Then I heard Daniel's voice again. "On belay," he shouted.

My hands shook, as I prepared to climb. For good luck, I stuck them in the chalk bag. "Maybe the chalk dust will put some magic in my hands," I wished. Then I called out, "Up rope." Daniel pulled up the slack until he felt the rope tug on my waist. "That's me," I shouted. Then, in a shaky voice, I yelled, "Climbing."

Daniel replied, "Go for it!" Then with a laugh he added, "Oops! I mean, climb away!"

Sweat broke out all over me. I talked constantly to myself. "Keep your feet spread apart on the open book. Don't lean into the crack. Here comes the first chock. Make sure you're balanced. Take out the chock and clip the carabiner onto your harness."

I focused so hard on the rock that I made it up the ledge without a slip. The ease of the climb startled me so much that I broke a rule. Instead of using a voice command, I called out: "Daniel, are you up there?"

"Can't hear you," he said in jest.

As I looked at the overhang, I decided what to yell back, "Watch me!" That told Daniel to anticipate a fall. It also told him that I was going for the overhang. I jammed my

feet and fingers into cracks and pulled my body up. Just over the overhang, I got a major surprise. My hand grabbed on a "bomber handhold," a knob that I could hold onto with all my strength.

As I pulled myself onto a thin edge, I caught my breath. That's when I saw Daniel's broad smile. "Just two more pieces of gear, Deb. Then you'll have finished your first 5.6 in a long time. Think you can make it?"

I flew to the top. My excitement at that minute still ranks with Kilimanjaro and other mountains I've climbed. I had broken through a wall of fear. I hugged Daniel and started talking rapidly. "I'm going to keep climbing, maybe three or four days a week. I'm going to get good enough to try a high altitude-rock climb."

Daniel laughed, "So what do you want to try?"

I thought for a second. My dad had just sent me a video on African volcanoes. "You've already done Kilimanjaro," said my father. "Which one are you going to do next?" I now shared my answer with Daniel, "Mount Kenya."

Daniel roared. "You're incredible. Two days ago, you couldn't get up a 5.3. Now you want to slap a rope on some volcano halfway around the world. But if you want to shoot for the top, I'll help you."

"When do you we get started?" I exclaimed.

Daniel relied, "Now. Let's go set up another climb." As I headed off with Daniel to find another route, I felt like I had taken my first steps back to East Africa.

Back to Africa

Daniel listened as I told him everything I had learned about Mount Kenya. "There are two peaks over 17,000 feet. One of them has ten levels. I've got to do lots of pitch climbing to build up my endurance. I've heard that there's a couple of traverses. So I'll need to practice moving sideways across ledges. It takes some people a full day to climb the highest summit. That means they've got to bivouac at the top. Can you imagine camping out on a rock summit that high? I'd better start climbing with a pack so that I can carry my own "bivy" gear. I've got to practice rappelling, too. Can you imagine looking over your shoulder before rappelling off a peak more than 17,000 feet high? It's going to be great!"

After hearing my wish list, Daniel responded, "We've got our work cut out for us. But the best training for climbing is climbing." And for nearly four months we climbed. Daniel worked a night shift. But he'd meet me mornings on rock faces near his home in Woodbury, Connecticut, about an hour from my house. On Daniel's days off, he'd meet me in Fishkill, New York. Together we'd head across the Hudson River to the Shawangunks (Gunks), just outside of New Paltz.

After about a month of climbing four and five times a week, Daniel said: "You getting cranked. You're using every muscle in your body." My body already knew that. I felt stiff nearly every morning. Calluses had sprouted on my hands. Bruises reminded me of the new moves that I had tried. Sometimes I made the move. And sometimes I fell. "Did you hurt yourself?" Daniel would shout. "Nah," I'd reply. "Just a few bruises." Every day felt like a mini-adventure.

My chance to head to East Africa came in the form of an announcement for an international social studies conference. Three nations—Kenya, Tanzania, and Uganda—hosted it. I'd get a chance to meet people interested in global education and a chance to climb the new mountain of my dreams. On top of that, I could visit with two good Kikuyu friends—Christina Mwangi and Lydiam Macharia. What more could I ask?

I soon found out the answer to that question. I needed to find a guide—somebody who'd climb one of the technical peaks with me. I wrote letters to climbing groups, asked people for names, and even searched on the Internet. Eventually, one of my letters landed with a small climbing group in Seattle. It traveled there by way of Tanzania. I had written to Wesley, my guide up

Kilimanjaro, who forwarded the letter to some of his friends in Washington. His friends couldn't climb with me. But they made dozens of calls trying to find somebody who could.

By this roundabout way, I finally turned up a guide who fit into my limited budget. I didn't know the person. Nor could I meet him. He had already headed for East Africa to work as a guide. But Wesley's friends had told the guide, whom I'll call B.P., about my requirements. "She wants to enjoy the mountain," they said. "She doesn't want to break any records for speed." They also told B.P., "She's coming to rock climb. She's been training for months." Finally they said, "We'll go over the gear list with her. We'll call another woman in Seattle who has already done the climb."

"The climb is really going to happen," I told Daniel in triumph. I think Daniel felt as good about it as I did. Somehow he found even more time to climb. He took me up 5.6 pitch climbs with weight on my back. And he got me up my first 5.7 with an overhang. "You're going to make it," he said.

Four days before I was due to take off, I had an accident. I had forgotten a basic climbing rule. I stopped watching the direction of the rope. Instead of staying under the anchor, I moved too far right. If I fell, I was in danger of becoming a human pendulum. And that's just what happened. My foot slipped off the edge, and I swung back toward the anchor. With no time to correct the swing, I slammed into the wall with the back of my head.

"Oh, no!" yelled Daniel. "I knew I should have made you wear a helmet." I touched the back of my head and felt a two-inch gash.

"I've got to get to Kenya," I said.

"First, you're going to a doctor," replied Daniel.

Daniel never left my side. He stood by while the doctors sewed four big blue stitches in my head. He also listened while I talked with the doctor. "Yes, you can still go to Kenya," said the doctor. "Yes, you can climb. But keep the stitches clean until you cut them out in five or six days. And, if you can be a little less of a rebel, try a helmet. It might save your life."

Two days later, Daniel and I went back up on the rocks. I wanted to make sure I wouldn't freeze. We did a solid 5.6 pitch climb in the Gunks. As a test, Daniel had me traverse, or cross, a ledge with a lot of exposure. I never panicked. At the end of the day, I exclaimed: "Great climb!"

I soon headed off to Nairobi, the capital of Kenya. My family and friends asked me to estimate when I'd leave Nairobi for the mountain. "I won't be with you physically," said Daniel. "But my thoughts will be with you."

"I'm nervous about this one," said my mother. "I think I'll ask your angels for a little extra help."

While in Nairobi, my Kikuyu friends arranged for me to do service. Christina, a doctor, took me to a street children's project—a shelter aimed at helping homeless young people. Here I volunteered my time as a nurse's aid.

Lydiam invited me to a *harambee*, which means "come together." Jomo Kenyatta, the driving force behind

Kenyan independence and the nation's first president, coined the term to urge Kenyans to help themselves. Today, Kenyans use the term to describe any community effort. Lydiam's harambee was held to start construction on a new church.

B.P. finally contacted me at my hotel. He came to my room to check over the gear. He started pulling out some of the gear that I routinely used. As he tossed items in a pile, he said: "Leave behind your belay plate. You'll use mine. It's a little different. But you'll figure it out. You won't need your chalk bag. Take out the nut pick, too."

I protested. "I use the nut pick to pull out gear when its stuck. I like my chalk bag. It's like a security blanket. Why do I have to learn new gear?"

B.P. said: "If you want to see how real mountaineers climb, I'm going to show you." B.P. had climbed Mount Kenya before, so I went along with his decision. But I didn't like it one bit.

The next day, we headed off to Mount Kenya. It lay in the Aberdare Highlands, one of the most fertile regions in East Africa. We traveled half the distance by "speed taxi," a taxi that makes no stops. Then we hired a four-wheel drive to make it the rest of the way. On the dirt road leading up to the mountain, foot-deep ruts nearly ended the climb before it started. Heavy chains on the wheels and a rut-dodging driver finally got us to the entrance of Mount Kenya National Park.

Mount Kenya was born three million years ago during the great upheaval that ripped apart East Africa and created the

Great Rift Valley. Geologists think this volcano once stood much higher than Kilimanjaro. But over the millennia, the forces of erosion have worn down the crater rim until all that remains are three peaks. They include a nontechnical peak named Point Lenana (16,355 feet) and two technical peaks named Nelion (17,022 feet) and Batian (17,340 feet).

We talked with other climbers on their way off the mountain. They gave us a weather report. "An ice storm knocked out Nelion," said one climber. "It's just too slick to get up. But Batian's still open." Their words determined our route. We were heading to Batian.

I set out with high expectations. But B.P. soon brought back bad memories of Pat, my climbing partner in Sikkim. He liked telling me what "real mountaineers" do. Taller than me, he had a longer stride. He moved up the trail much faster, while I struggled to keep up. If I complained, he'd say, "Real mountaineers have to get up the peaks quickly."

B.P. also liked controlling the food and water. Small-sized people burn food more quickly when they climb (or do any kind of exercise). To keep my energy high, I've learned to eat regular snacks and drink lots of water. I constantly had to remind B.P not to head off without leaving behind some food or telling me where I could find water. He also had the route map. (He told me to leave mine back in the hotel.) I was, in a word, made to feel dependent. And I hated it.

Besides needing B.P. for food, water, and the map, I also needed him for the rock climb. Unlike Pat, he had more than twenty years experience in the mountains. He was a proven climber. So I tried to get along with him. I told B.P., "I rely on your judgment on how far we go up the mountain. But I want to try it. When are we going to get there?" "Soon," he answered. "But first I want to do some rope work with you. I've got a site in mind."

I felt uneasy. I wondered why we weren't doing the rope work at the foot of Batian. I got even more nervous when we set up camp in a small basin, rather than near a climbing area. After lunch, B.P. bought out his climbing rope and handed me one end. "This is a test," he said. "Let me see how fast you can tie a figure eight." The word "test" made me pause. "You'll have to do better than that if you want to climb Bation," he said. "We need to climb fast to get up ten pitches."

Next, B.P pointed to a boulder. "Put on your harness. I want to see how you rappel off the top." A queasy feeling settled over me, especially when I saw nettle bushes around the base of the boulder.

"Why are we doing this?" I asked.

"I want to see what I'm climbing with," said B.P.

"Then let's climb some real rocks," I shot back. I stomped off to the tent, saying "End of today's test."

The next day, we reached Batian. As I stared up at its peak, I felt overwhelmed. This is what Daniel and I had trained for. "I want to try it," I told B.P.

He then said the awful words: "In my judgment, I don't think you can do it."

"All I want is a chance to try," I said. "I don't need to

make it to the top." After arguing, B.P. agreed to lead one climb.

B.P. kept his promise. But I felt set up. He chose to lead a climb late in the day. The sun hung low in the sky, and temperatures had already begun to drop. B.P. pointed to a site along the edge of Batian where we'd climb. A huge pile of boulders separated us from the site. B.P. bounded over the boulders as quickly as he could. I yelled out, "Hey, why are you going so fast?"

He shot off, "If you were a real mountaineer, you'd know we should be far apart in case I set off a rock slide."

I didn't know if that was true. But I knew that if I moved too fast, I risked hurting myself in a fall. And I still had to get off the mountain.

When I caught up with B.P., he had already strapped on his rack and begun selecting gear. "This is a 5.6," he said. "But an African 5.6. is a lot harder than a U.S. 5.6. It's typical of the crux at the top. Let's see if you can make it."

I put on my harness and climbing shoes. Meanwhile, B.P. started to place gear without the protection of a belayer. (Although I don't do it, some very experienced climbers go up routes that are well within their abilities without a belayer.) When he reached a level about 40 feet off the ground, he set up a belay. I quickly tied in, called out the basic climbing commands, and then started heading up.

After the smooth granite of the Gunks, I welcomed the little bumps and edges on Batian's volcanic rock. I found little handholds all over. The rubber on my shoes seemed to stick better to the rugged surface. When I joined B.P. on a ledge, he said: "You made it up pretty fast. But I was wrong about the level. It's about a 5.4. Plus you're wearing your climbing shoes. You should be able to do this climb in hiking boots."

I held my temper until we rappelled down. I told B.P., "I talked to people about gear before I left. I wanted every advantage on this climb—including the stickiest shoes possible. A woman climber from Seattle went to the top using these same kind of shoes. She doubled socks to fight the cold. I stretched these shoes to do the same. You're just looking for excuses not to take me on the rocks!"

When I got back into the camp, I sat on a rock and stared at the peak. "I just wanted to try," I whispered. I felt angry, hurt, and cheated. But there was nothing I could do about it.

If you hire a guide, you pay the guide's fees and expenses long before you arrive at the climb. There's no way to get the money back if the climb doesn't turn out as you hoped. That's part of the deal. A more important part of the deal is the authority a guide exercises on a climb itself. A guide is something like a harbor pilot who must bring a vessel safely into port. The pilot's word is final, overruling even the decision of a captain or the ship's owner. On a mountain, a guide is responsible for getting you safely up and down the peak. And his or her word is final, too. For whatever reason, B.P. did not think I could make the technical climb up Batian. I disliked B.P., and I disagreed with him. But it was his decision to make, and the decision was final.

We now climbed Mount Kenya's nontechnical route up to Point Lenana's 16,355-foot summit. With as many eco-zones as Kilimanjaro, the landscape of Mount Kenya is startling in its variety and power. So I decided to focus on the mountain's stark beauty—from mist-filled mountain passes to turquoise glacial lakes called tarns. I also looked forward to summit day and another chance to stand on a tropical glacier.

While traveling to Lenana, I took advantage of an opportunity to learn more about the Kikuyu by interviewing the porters. A porter named Munuhe (moon AH hay) had attended college. One night, he invited me to share supper with a group of porters from several different climbs. Not only did I have some good food, including a cabbage-like dish called *ugali*, but I got some great stories. I also made a friend. Munuhe and I still write to each other.

Near the end of the climb, I went over all the events that had led me to Mount Kenya. The best climbs of the past year, I realized, had been right in my own backyard. I laughed recalling how Daniel had coaxed me up the rocks. What a contrast to B.P.! I thought. He couldn't do enough to keep me *off* the rocks. Then I thought of something a friend had written to me in a letter: "The only peace that you find in the mountains is the peace that you bring there." I had let my expectations of climbing Mount Kenya soar higher than the mountain itself. That's why my disappointment felt so bitter. "I love mountains," I said. "It's enough that I'm here." With these words, the peace returned.

After coming home, I talked about my experiences on the mountain with many climbers. "Not getting up one of the peaks doesn't make you less of a climber," said Daniel. "Let's go to the Gunks and prove it." I also listened to the tough judgment calls shared by people who had led climbs. I thought, Who knows what decisions you might have to make someday?

A woman climber taught me the most important lesson of all. "As we become more confident," she said, "we realize that we have the right to pick who we climb with. Climbing is a love that we have to share only with a friend." I promised myself that someday I'd return to Mount Kenya to climb Batian with a friend.

I expect to meet this friend in the mountains. I've already met a lot of people with whom I'd like to travel. Their stories make me want to keep climbing—to add chapters to my own climbing story. By trading tales, we can say "I understand why you climb. I've had similar adventures, similar disappointments, and similar fears. And, like you, I keep heading back."

Tales from the Trails

Did I ever tell you about the time I moonwalked in Sikkim? One night, just before I set off to climb Kanchenjunga, a fourteen-year-old named Pema Namygal knocked on the door of my hotel room. "Turn on your television," said Pema. "We just moved the satellite disk on the hotel, so we can beam in M-TV." As the screen flickered, a rapper from India came into view. "That's Apache Indian," proclaimed Pema. "He's hot here." He then added, "I write rap, too. In fact, I have a rap name. It's Kool MC. Can you moonwalk?" With that, he started dancing, and so did I.

Did I ever tell you about the time I met an eight-year-old climber on Mount Kenya? His name is Ross Finley, and he traveled to Africa to climb the mountain with his dad. I met Ross while camping outside a trekking hut at 13,000 feet. "How do you like climbing?" I asked Ross.

"The mountain's okay," he answered. "But I don't like the

rats that get into the trekking huts. They try to eat my food."

Later, after I sent some photos to Ross, his dad, Ian Finley, wrote to me. Said Ian: "Ross had a great climb. Compared to me, he's a little goat. No altitude sickness and no real exhaustion. I think it's great for such a young kid to have tackled such a big mountain early in life. He's hooked!"

Climbing has filled my life with stories. In addition to my own stories, I collect the stories of other climbers. I especially like the stories that come from out of nowhere—the ones told to me as I wander far from the mountains.

I found out about one climber in a local pizza shop. I always send postcards of my climbs to the people who work there. After I climbed Kilimanjaro, the owner Mike announced: "I've got a friend who really wants to meet you. He's climbed 42 of the highest mountains in New York. His name is Bob Mattice."

Bob wanted to talk to me about Kilimanjaro—his dream climb. But I wanted to find out about a mountain-climbing challenge in my own area. By talking with Bob, I learned about a club called the Adirondack 46ers. Its members have climbed all 46 peaks above 4,000 feet in the Adirondacks of northeastern New York. Since the club was founded, satellite photos have revealed that four of the peaks are a little less than 4,000 feet. But you have to climb them nevertheless to be in the club.

It took Bob fourteen years of weekend climbing, but, in

1995, he climbed his 46th peak. "How do you feel?" I asked Bob.

He replied: "At first, I felt sad. I wondered, 'After you accomplish this, where do you go next?' But then I came up with a new scheme. There are 111 mountains in the Northeast region—including New York—over 4,000 feet. So I'm going to try to climb them all." He added with a smile, "It may even be a family project. My wife, Barbara, has already climbed 2 mountains. My ten-year-old son, Brendan, has climbed 7. And, with luck, my eight-year-old daughter, Caitlyn, will soon climb her first mountain. It's great when you share a kindred spirit with your own children."

Another local climber—this time from Westport, Connecticut—came my way while I visited a mapmaker in connection with a writing assignment for a magazine. "You must talk with the shopkeeper below my studio," he said. "Her daughter just climbed Mount Baker."

Abigail Griffith tackled this 10,761-foot peak the summer after she graduated ninth grade. Mount Baker—the third highest peak in Washington State—wears a heavy coat of ice fed by a dozen glaciers. Abi had already done two prior wilderness expeditions at ages fourteen and fifteen. In 1993, her good friend Mike Arron had summited both Mount Rainier and Mount Baker at age fifteen. He convinced Abi to try traveling up ice. In 1994, at age sixteen, Abi joined a youth expedition heading for Baker.

The group spent two days learning self-arrest techniques before climbing the mountain. Said Abi, "It's a neat feeling to fall on the snow and to stop yourself or somebody else with just one jam of the icc ax into the glacier." She then recalled, "While practicing, we crossed a snow bridge. As my friend Sasha put all her weight on her right foot and ice ax, her left foot slipped into the crevasse. Two other people on the team immediately went down in self arrest. I thought, Yes! That's how you do it! Instead of feeling scared, I felt safe."

To combat fatigue, the team leaders—two experienced guides—told the young people to imagine themselves as some kind of animal. Abi chose an ant. "An ant can carry something like ten times its weight," explained Abi. "And their feet stick to walls. Whenever I got tired, I just thought of a little ant climbing some huge wall, and I took a few more steps."

All the steps added up, and Abi reached the summit. "It was so small, we had to take turns standing on it," recalled Abi. "Standing on a little pile of rocks was not the highlight of the climb. For me, it was climbing down a steep wall of snow called the Roman Wall and crossing over a crevasse at its base. It was pretty exciting."

Later Abi got a chance to practice climbing out of a crevasse. After setting up an anchor, the team lowered her into a gaping hole in the glacier. "It's so beautiful when you're in there by choice," said Abi. "I looked up and saw a wall of white on each side of me. Below was nothing but darkness. Everything was very, very quiet except for the trickling of water. It was really neat!"

The climb changed Abi. "That summer," she explained,

was the happiest I've ever been. I found something I want to keep doing for the rest of my life."

In addition to stories of local climbers, I collect the stories of people met during my travels. Once while climbing a mountain in Mexico, I shared a trekking hut with a group of mountaineering students from Prescott College (located in Prescott, Arizona). I spent part of the evening talking to one of the students—twenty-two-year-old Erik Van Sinderen from Lafayette, California.

I asked Erik to describe his favorite climb. He chose a 220-foot sea stack—a needle of rock sticking straight out of the ocean—named the Old Man of Stoerd. It lies just off the northwest coast of England. Erik went there as part of a climbing course offered by Prescott College. The team included six young men, one young woman, and an instructor with an artificial leg. "My teacher was such a great climber," said Erik. "You wouldn't know about his leg unless he told you."

On the day of the climb, clouds rolled in and an approaching storm kicked up the ocean. But the team decided to go for the sea stack nonetheless. Explained Erik: "We set up a Tyrolian Traverse—a kind of tight rope—anchored between a cliff at the edge of the shore and to the 'old man' in the ocean. My friend Max stripped down and swam 15 feet against the tide to carry the rope out to the sea stack. Once the traverse was set up, the rest of us clipped our harnesses onto the rope with carabiners. Then, hanging underneath the rope by our waists, we used our hands to pull ourselves across the waves."

The instructor broke the climbers into two teams. One would lead, the other would follow. Erik was on the lead team. As he headed up the limestone pinnacle, rain squalls hit. "We were very exposed over crazy waves," recalled Erik. "We headed in and out of chimneys—cracks big enough to fit your body into. But the chimneys were so wet, I felt like they'd spit me out at any second. Whenever I pulled myself from a chimney, these birds called fulmars screeched in my face. It was wild!"

Both teams made it to the top, rappelled off the sea stack, and pulled themselves back across the Tyrolian Traverse. "Muddy and soaking wet," said Erik, "we hugged each other, saying over and over 'Great climb!' Great climb!'"

While working on this book, I asked Tom Nickels, who has helped me to arrange some of my climbs, to tell me his favorite climbing story. Tom chose a climb up Kilimanjaro. But he described a route very different from the one that I took. Along with Scott Fisher—a mountaineer who has summited such famous peaks as K-2 in Pakistan and Lhotse and Everest in Nepal—Tom climbed the Heime Glacier.

Tom works for Scott, who is the co-owner of a small Seattle-based mountaineering company called Mountain Madness. In late 1994, Scott and Tom led a group partway up the Shira route—the one I took—and then turned the group over to a Tanzanian guide. With a single client, they set out to find the glacier. "We used a guidebook written in 1986 or 1987," said Tom. "When we got to the glacier, we found that it had receded. What had been a moderate climb now looked more severe."

Scott and Tom felt the three-person team could handle the steeper route. So they grabbed a couple hours of sleep, and at midnight started up the glacier. "It was cold," recalled Tom. "But the moon was shining, and conditions looked good for the climb."

The receding glacier, however, created a surprise. One of the steepest pitches had turned into a vertical climb of half ice, half crumbling volcanic rock. Scott went up first, then the client. "When my turn came," said Tom, "I felt pretty good on the ice. But I'd only been climbing about a year. I'd never switched so dramatically between ice and rock before. When I reached the rock part, I hooked an ice ax into what I thought was a solid piece of rock. But when I pulled on it, the pick flew out and the other end crashed into my forehead. I'd attached an ice ax to each of my wrists with a band. I let the axes dangle from the bands. Then, with blood pouring into my right eye, I climbed to the top with my hands."

Scott administered first aid. But there was no turning back. Explained Tom, "We climbed 100-foot pitches of ice and crossed some of the most punishing scree I've ever seen. I pushed limits that I'd never dreamed of. Yet somehow we got to the summit ahead of schedule. Most people make it up the Heime Glacier in two and a half days. We did it in one long, exhausting day. I stared down from the summit and saw the rest of the group camped at 18,500 feet. I felt incredible. This one climb had pulled together all my skills—rope handling, ice climbing, rock climbing, and more. I knew now I'd be ready to handle my next big climb—Mount McKinley in the spring of 1995."

Tom made it possible for me to hear another incredible story, this time from Stacy Allison, one of Scott Fisher's close friends. I especially wanted to talk to Stacy. Like me, she's small—5 feet 3 inches and 110 pounds. Yet Stacy was the first U.S. woman to climb Mount Everest, the world's biggest mountain.

Stacy doesn't come from a climbing family. But the seeds for climbing were planted as a child. As Stacy told me in one conversation, "When I used to ski near Mount Hood, Oregon, I always thought, someday I'll climb that mountain. That dream led me up Mount Hood and a whole lot of other mountains."

Stacy took her first climb at age nineteen when a friend asked her to go rock climbing in Utah's Zion National Park. "I knew almost immediately," recalled Stacy, "that I wanted to become a climber. I was gung-ho from the start. Whenever I met a good climber, I wanted to learn whatever he or she knew."

"Are there any differences between men and women climbers?" I asked Stacy.

"The only difference I notice is size," she answered. "Men can carry heavier packs. But with altitude climbing, gender doesn't make a lick of difference. It all comes down to technique, endurance, and ability to handle thin air."

To find out how Stacy handled Mount Everest, you can

read her book *Beyond the Limits*. But, like most mountaineers, Stacy has a lot of other stories to tell. When I
asked Stacy to pick her favorite story, she thought about it
for several days. She finally chose a 1981 climb up Mount
Robson—the highest peak in the Canadian Rockies.

Stacy climbed Mount Robson's 2,000-foot North Face—
a technical rock climb—in a single day. She and her partner Curt wanted to climb light, so they left behind their
sleeping bags. They planned to spend a cold night at the
top and then head down another route the next morning.
But morning brought a raging blizzard. "We could hardly
see," said Stacy. "Our only saving grace was that other people had tried to get out just ahead of us. Every now and
then, we spotted a footprint in the snow."

The footprints led to a 45-degree ice face. Stacy
described what happened next. "I downclimbed first. I
faced howling winds, blinding snow, and nightfall. For the
skills that I had at that time, I was definitely on the edge.
I tried to screw gear into the ice, but huge ice chunks kept
coming down and hitting me. It hurt. I couldn't figure out
what was taking Curt so long. I was hungry, cold, scared,
and in a lot of pain. For a fleeting second, I thought: I can
cut the rope and jump off. Then I won't be in pain anymore. In a flash, I realized: Ah, ha! This is how climbers
die. They just give up. Wow! I have a choice. I can choose
to give up and die. Or I can choose to get through the pain
and live. I chose to live."

When Curt caught up, Stacy learned that a broken ice ax
had slowed him down. Together they continued the

121

descent until they got to a flat glacier. Here they dug a small pit and shivered through the night. The two climbers got off the mountain—alive.

"I learned a lot from that climb," Stacy told me. "It taught me that I don't have to give up, not only on climbs but in life. When I want to sit down and rest, I go a few more feet. Those few feet can mean the difference between life and death on a mountain or success and defeat in life."

Through Tom Nickels, I met another experienced climber named Mark Gunlogson. Mark, a native of Seattle, took his first climbing course at age fifteen. Then he and a couple of friends headed into the Cascades on their own. "It was kind of trial by fire," explained Mark. "We didn't have licenses. So we asked our parents to drive us to climbing places. We'd hang on the rocks until they'd pick us up."

I asked Mark to recall how he felt as a teenage rock climber. "Pretty good," replied Mark. "I never liked team sports, but I like athletics. Rock climbing allowed me to engage in a physical sport without being competitive. Besides, it felt natural to be in the mountains. I knew I belonged there."

I eventually asked Mark to tell me his favorite story. "Wow, I don't know," he replied. "I've done a lot of climbs all over the world that other people think are noteworthy. But the one that sticks out in my mind is a very obscure route in a rock-climbing area outside of Seattle called Index. I did about a 4,000-foot climb that involved sustained technical skill for more than thirteen hours. Other people may not care. But it meant a lot to me—especially the descent. I slid down a snowbank, put in my last anchor, and literally ran out of rope. I was hanging some 20 feet off the ground when I went down the rope and jumped. Luckily, I landed in a snow bank instead of on the rocks."

Mark has done peaks well over 23,000 feet. So I asked, "Why did you pick this as your favorite story?"

He replied, "Because it called for total commitment from me. You don't need some big route in the Himalayas or the Andes for a good climb. It all comes down to an individual's best shot. If my total commitment is 5.10 and your total commitment is 5.6, they're both the same. Climbing should come down to you, not competition with somebody else."

Mark's attitude makes him a good teacher and climbing partner for me. And, as you will see, that's what he became in 1994 and 1995.

13

A La Cumbre (To the Summit)

"Want to boil some water for fun?" asked Mark.

"What are the other choices?" I laughed.

"Well, we could count the little squares in the fabric of our tent," he replied. "That's what I did when a snowstorm on Mount McKinley kept me in my tent for nearly four days."

With a mock moan, I responded, "We've only been in our tent for four hours. What will we do for an encore?"

Mark and I had just finished the first day of a three-day climb on Mount Rainier, the highest peak in Washington State and in the entire Cascade Mountains. We'd set up camp around 4:00 P.M. when a combination of sunset and snow squalls had made it too dark to travel. It was only early November, 1994. But more than 5 feet of snow had already fallen on the lower portion of Rainier.

I had come to Washington to do glacier training. With the exception of Alaska, Washington has the largest sys-

124

tem of glaciers of any state in the United States. Mount Rainier alone boasts some 35 square miles of ice. I wanted to practice walking on ice with crampons—steel devices with multiple sharp teeth that are attached to the soles of special climbing boots. Each boot is really two boots: a stiff outer boot to keep out water and a lighter inner boot to keep in heat. Designed for technical ice climbing or high-altitude expeditions, the boots' rigid construction makes them ideal for holding crampons in place. But at about 2 pounds each, they look and feel like moon boots.

While on the glaciers, I also wanted to learn how to cross crevasses—cracks in a glacier's surface that can extend downward just a few inches or for more than 150 feet. But suppose I didn't make it across a crevasse? Or suppose a crevasse hidden beneath the snow swallowed me or my partner as we walked across it? To handle such potential dangers, I needed to learn crevasse rescue—the techniques for arresting a fall and for climbing out of ice crevices.

I knew when I set out for Washington that a snowstorm might knock out glacier training. Fresh snow can hide crevasses, wipe out trails, and create whiteouts—conditions in which snow or fog decreases visibility to near zero. Mark and I had an alternate plan. If a storm hit, we'd still try to get onto a mountain so that I could experience the severe weather conditions that face climbers on most high-altitude expeditions. Among other things, a climber can expect short days, extremes in hot and cold, snow blindness, and "burnout" from hauling a lot of extra gear and breaking new trails in the snow.

Mount Rainier, maintained as a national park since 1899, has a well-established park service that keeps the mountain open for much of the year. When a snowstorm in fact closed a lot of peaks in the Cascades, Mark and I headed to Rainier. Instead of traveling on crampons, I'd lug around my pack on snowshoes. I'd also learn to camp in winter conditions. As Mark had explained, "On some expeditions, like McKinley, you'll be living in snow for almost three weeks."

Weather forecasts indicated up to a foot of snow a day on parts of Rainier. We registered our route and expected date of return with the park service—a necessary precaution on any climb, especially a winter climb. We then set off up the mountain. I found it hard to believe that I didn't sink up to my neck in the snow. But my snowshoes carried me—and a 45-pound pack—up the trail.

Mark picked a good campsite for our first night on the mountain. It lay just off one of the park's designated trails—well-traveled routes clearly indicated on a map. A string of pine trees provided shelter from the wind. A flat area adjacent to the trees offered a level base for a tent. Nearby, a swift-running stream had not yet frozen solid. That saved us from using time and fuel to melt snow or ice. However, at tree-level altitudes, animal feces still seep into streams and ponds. So we had to boil drinking water or purify it with iodine tablets to kill giardia—a bacteria that can cause vomiting and diarrhea.

During the first four hours in the tent, we'd cooked supper (brown rice and lentils), planned our next day's activities, and climbed into our sleeping bags. Mark had used his skis to pack down the snow on the tent site. But the weight of my body still made little hollows. "Punch down the snow until it's level," Mark had directed. "You'll get comfortable soon."

Snow pelted the tent. Mark had used our ski poles to flag the location of gear outside the tent. From time to time, he hit the side of the tent with his hand or foot to knock off the snow. "You don't want the tent to collapse on us, do you?" he joked. Then he added, "We'll take turns shoveling a path around the tent so we can get out."

As I swallowed a couple of gulps of water, I asked: "So where's the bathroom?"

"You have two choices," said Mark. "You can use a bottle or crawl out the back."

"I'll take the back," I replied. "Then you'd better dig a snow latrine," Mark smiled. "Without your snowshoes, you'll sink so deep into the snow that I'll have to drag you out." Grumbling, I unzipped the tent flap, plunged into waist-deep snow, and started shoveling.

The payback was the beautiful whiteness of the night. So was the soft glow of Mark's headlamp inside the tent. The night seemed peaceful and safe. It's going to be a good couple of days, I thought. And it was.

Besides seeing the incredible beauty of Mount Rainier in winter, I learned some basic principles of snow avalanches. "There are two kinds of avalanches," explained Mark, "loose-snow avalanches and slab avalanches." He then described each one. "Loose-snow avalanches begin when snow crystals slide down a slope and pick up speed and snow along the way. Slab avalanches start when a solid chunk of snow breaks off. Both types of avalanches are caused by unstable snow—snow that's not well bonded to a hillside, underlying snow layers, or other snow crystals."

Mark showed me how to use a shovel and the snow probe on my ski pole to check snow layers. He pointed out the size of snow crystals in each layer as well as the way in which layers adhered to each other. He then went over other factors that contribute to avalanches—the steepness or curve of slopes, the lack of natural anchors such as trees or rocks, changing weather conditions, and so on.

Later, in the tent, Mark pulled out a contour map of Mount Rainier. "Do you know how to read a contour map?" he asked.

"Sure," I replied. "Where lines are closer together, the land is steeper. Where they're farther apart, the land is gentler."

"Good," he responded. "Now show me where you're least likely to get hit by an avalanche." Two routes proved the safest: the tops of ridges away from overhangs and valleys far from the bottom of slopes.

"In plotting a route across heavy snow," said Mark, "always check the lay of the land. It can save your life."

Impressed by Mark's knowledge, I asked: "What are you doing later this winter? Any chance we can still find a glacier to climb?" He laughed.

"How much time have you got?"

I said, "I can only take about five days off from work. What can we do with it?"

"Well, Deb," replied Mark, "we can head to Mexico. I know a couple of volcanoes that have some good glaciers that we could climb in January. Are you interested?"

Mark didn't have to ask twice. By the time we left Rainier, we had made a date to climb Popocatépetl—a volcano about 50 miles southeast of Mexico City. The climb promised everything I wanted—an altitude of 17,930 feet and glacier routes that required use of crampons and an ice ax. If I handled the altitude well, I even had a shot at "Popo's" twin peak, a 17,160-foot volcano called Iztaccuccíhuatl, or "Ixta."

I booked a super bargain $240 round-trip airline ticket to Mexico City. Aside from bus tickets and a $17-a-night room in the Mexican capital, we expected to keep costs down by staying in a tent and eating trail food. "It's going to happen," I told everyone who'd listen. "I'm finally heading up ice with weight on my back."

At the end of December, a major glitch occurred. Popo lived up to the translation of its Aztec name—"Smoking Mountain"—and sent a cloud of volcanic ash spewing into the sky. The Mexican government evacuated some 70,000 people from nearby villages and sealed off routes leading to both Popo and Ixta.

I called Mark in Seattle. "Have we got a Plan B?" I asked.

"It's too late and too expensive to change our airline

tickets," said Mark. "But if you're willing to lose two days in travel, we can head east to El Pico de Orizaba. It's the second highest peak in North America. We won't have any time to acclimatize. And we'll have to head up fast. I give us a 50-50 shot of making it. Do you still want to try?" "A fifty percent shot is better than no shot at all," I responded enthusiastically. "Let's go for it!"

Two weeks later, Mark and I met in Mexico City. We loaded up on bottled water and traveled by bus to the village of Tlachichuca—the last stop before heading up Orizaba. Here we stayed at a climbing dormitory run by the Reyes family. Our host, Señor Reyes, arranged for an army truck to carry us over the rut-filled roads leading to the base of the mountain. As a practicing physician, Señor Reyes also warned us of potential dangers—fast altitude gain and hard ice. "We lost a climber not more than two days ago," said Señor Reyes. "He broke a crampon and fell down the glacier. The mountain can be very dangerous."

Mark had climbed Orizaba before—and a whole lot of other mountains. He thanked Señor Reyes for his advice. Then he spoke with me in private. "We're going to be pushing envelopes the whole way, Deb. But somebody's got to give you a measure so that you can decide if you want to push higher and harder. I'll draw the line at all unacceptable risks. But, otherwise, you carry your weight the whole way. Just remember one thing—on ice there is no room for error. If either of us falls, we're both in a lot of trouble."

Bumping on the road up to the mountain, many

thoughts passed through my mind. My last two climbs—
to the base camp of Sikkim's Kanchenjunga and up one of
the peaks on Mount Kenya—had brought disappointment. I tried to keep my hopes in line. But even mediation
failed to calm my excitement. I wanted to climb.

We arrived in late afternoon at a stone building called
the Octavio Alvarez hut. We dropped our gear on some
wooden bunks. Then Mark had me hike up and down
some trails so he could check my pulse rate. It went up to
nearly 100 beats a minute, but returned to a normal rate
of around 80 in less than minute. "You're okay," said
Mark. "You recover pretty quick, even though you've had
no time to acclimatize. At altitude the heart beats faster
than at sea level, you know. It's got to work overtime to get
oxygen pumped to the brain."

For supper, we drank a lot of liquids—soup, juice,
water, and cocoa—to hydrate ourselves. Mark also went
over our climb. The next day, we'd set up a high camp at
16,000 feet, where we'd spend the night. Then, if neither
us were sick, we'd push for the summit. After tagging the
18,410 peak, we'd return to the high camp, tear it down,
and come off the mountain in one long, exhausting day.

To reduce weight in my pack, I wore my double ice
boots up the mountain. Walking in rigid boots over scree
with a heavy pack proved a real balancing act. I held my
ice ax by its head and used it as a cane. Even so, by the
time we reached the first glacier, I felt tired. Mark had a
difficult decision to make—cross a short stretch of glacier
to another scree path or head straight up the glacier.

"What do you want to do?" he asked.

"I hate scree," I answered. "I'm ready to try the ice, if you're ready to show me."

Mark thought—but not for long. "Put on your crampons and harness," he directed. "We're going to simul-climb up the glacier." That meant we'd be tied together by rope. Mark would lead, and I'd follow.

After checking my harness and crampons, Mark went over what's known as the "French technique." With each step, I had to slam ten of the twelve points on the crampon into the ice. Only the two front points stayed free, so that they wouldn't get stuck when the rest of the foot was lifted up. Depending on the slope of the ice, I had to know how to position my feet. On low-angled ice, I walked flat-footed, with my toes pointed out, duck fashion. On steep-angled ice, I sidestepped uphill diagonally. I also had to remember to jam the point of my ice ax into the glacier when my feet were balanced. In this way, I'd have an anchor when I stepped out of balance. (You need to learn these techniques from an experienced climber.)

Mark watched me take the first few steps. Then he headed up the glacier. The ice looked like a glassy carpet, and, like glass, it was slippery. As I slammed my feet in the ice, I felt my muscles strain. Walking on crampons can tire your legs fast. But I felt more stable than on the rocky scree. "I like traveling over ice," I called out.

"Well, don't get too used to it," answered Mark. "You've still got a couple of hours of scree climbing at the end of the glacier."

By the time we set up a high camp, I felt exhausted. I barely wanted to eat. But at altitude, that's dangerous. So I forced down soup and a roll. Because of the fast ascent—2,500 feet in one day—Mark suggested we protect ourselves against altitude sickness. Mark had never taken Diamox. But before we went to sleep, we each took a half of a tablet. "We don't have an extra day to get sick," said Mark. "Set your alarm for 4:00 A.M.," he added. "Then you won't have to be so nervous about your pace. We'll have plenty of time."

My alarm never went off. We woke up around 8:30 A.M. and no longer had plenty of time to make it to the summit. Mark decided to go for the top nonetheless. But he gave me three hours to do it. "Take most of the weight out of your pack," he directed. "We can't have it slow you down." We then made our way to the glacier that led to the summit.

For hour after hour, I jammed my crampons in the snow and ice. Clouds rolled in and produced a near whiteout. Flags and scattered footprints guided us. But I never glimpsed the summit. My aching muscles told me I'd never complete the climb. Every time I thought I couldn't take another step, I'd call out: "How far? I can't go much longer." Like Columbus, Mark would answer: "Just a little longer. The summit's just ahead."

At 11:30, I yelled, "My time's up. We have to turn back."

"I lied," said Mark. "You have until noon." And by noon we indeed reached the edge of the crater—the so-called false summit.

Mark signaled for me to sit beside him. He pointed to a rock peak off to the right. "There's the true summit," he said. "But you've done enough. We've got to get off this mountain, too. So rest for a few minutes. Then we're heading down."

As I lay back on the ground, Mark started yelling: "*A la cumbre! A la cumbre!*" "What's that mean?" I asked.

"To the summit," he said, laughing. "We're going for the summit."

"What about getting down?" I asked.

"I'm a good mountaineer," answered Mark. "I'll get us out of here."

"Is *that* the truth?" I asked.

"Yea, that's really the truth," he replied. "But it's going to take all of your strength to do it."

I felt good reaching the false summit. But I felt great making it to the true summit. I may be a journeyer, but I still like to complete some of the journeys. "All right!" I yelled. Mark pulled out a camera and took a picture. Then he said, "Let's get out of here. The lack of oxygen is killing a few of our brain cells each minute. Besides, we need to get off the ice before the sun sets."

No climb is over until you're off the mountain. And, for me, getting off the Orizaba was tough. I had to descend two glaciers and huge stretches of scree. At the last glacier, Mark made another judgment call. "You're tired. But I trust you more on the ice than on the scree. I'll anchor you while you start down. You're going first."

By the time we hit the lower scree field, the sun had set.

I felt like laying down on the rocks and sleeping. But I switched on my headlamp instead. About an hour into the night, Mark spotted a bonfire at the base of the mountain. "It's the driver sent by Señor Reyes," he said. "He's built a beacon to guide us. I'm going ahead, so I can make voice contact. Watch your step."

With about 100 yards to go, Mark rejoined me.

"I can't move," I said.

"It's okay," he answered. "I'll take your pack. You're ready to walk off this mountain."

At Octavio Alvarez hut, a group of four climbers congratulated us. "Mark did it," I told them. And in fact, I couldn't have made the climb without him. He looked at me. "You don't know what you've done, do you?"

"Tell me," I replied.

"You just pushed yourself up and down more than 18,000 feet of rock and ice with a heavy pack on your back. And you did in two days with no acclimatization. Pretty good, Deb."

Tired and elated, I asked: "Will you climb with me again?"

"Sure," said Mark. "How about doing some crevasse rescue training in Peru? Maybe we can even climb Huascaran. At 22,205 feet, it's the second tallest mountain in South America. Are you up for it?"

I knew at that moment that I'd not only climb in Peru, but in every part of the world to which I could travel. And if I couldn't travel, I'd climb in the mountains near my home. But one way or the other, I'd keep climbing and keep chasing the magic.

Epilogue—So You Want to Be a Climber

Who says you can't be a climber? It all starts with a wish: "I wish that was me on that mountain." You might be thinking, "But I'm afraid of heights." Training and trust in a partner teach you to overcome that fear. Once you break down the fear of falling, it's easier to face other fears. That's part of the magic of climbing. It helps you become less afraid of life's other challenges.

Now you might be thinking. Okay, I can handle the fear of falling. But I'm still not good enough to be a climber. I'm too small. I'm too big. I'm too clumsy. But look at me. I'm small and dyslexic. Nobody would call me the world's best climber. Sometimes I fall on the rocks, and sometimes I don't get to the summit. Yet each time I head onto a rock face or up a mountain, I learn something new about climbing—and, more importantly, about myself. That's part of the magic of climbing, too. It changes you. Instead of worrying about failing, you start saying, "I'll give it a shot." What have I got to lose?

Maybe now you're thinking, I don't have the money to start climbing. But all you need to begin is a good pair of sneakers or hiking boots. Try hiking some wilderness trails. Or do some bouldering—climbing along boulders or small cliffs close to the ground. Practice teamwork by having a friend or relative spot you—stand behind you—in case you slip.

When you're ready to start learning some technical skills, go to a climbing store and price used climbing shoes. (Climbers trade in shoes for better ones.) Make sure there's lots of untorn rubber left on the soles. You might spend $35 to $50 dollars for used shoes. If you buy new shoes, don't get top of the line. (New climbers tend to drag their feet along the rocks. So they scrape up the rubber pretty fast.) My first pair of new climbing shoes cost $90.

Your only other purchase might be a climbing harness for about $30 to $40. Your climbing teacher will have the rest of the gear. If you fall in love with climbing, as I hope you will, add to your equipment little by little. For my birthdays, family and friends ask me to circle gear in a climbing catalog. It all adds up.

Those of you who don't live near any mountains might be thinking, "I don't have any place to climb." But before you rule out climbing, check gyms in your area. Climbing has become so popular that many fitness clubs and schools have built climbing walls—thick pieces of plywood with handholds and footholds attached. My local high school has one. So do I. My dad put it up in my backyard.

To show you how the magic of climbing can touch the lives of all kinds of young people, I saved one of my favorite stories for last. It involves a nonprofit climbing organization called Project U.S.E. (U.S.E. stands for Urban Suburban Environments.) Instead of the mountains, it began in the industrial cities of New Jersey—places such as Trenton and Newark.

I found out about Project U.S.E. while climbing Orizaba in Mexico. Here I met Chris Black, one of the climbing instructors at Arizona's Prescott College. "You won't believe this," Chris told me, "but I once worked for a climbing group that started in the inner cities of New Jersey. You've got to talk to Phil Costello, one of the group's founders. He'll have lots of stories for you."

I called Phil as soon as I got back home. First, I asked Phil about himself. I discovered that he had begun climbing while in the Marines. "I was hooked right away," he recalled. I also learned that Phil had worked with Outward Bound—a national organization that takes inner-city youths into the wilderness.

It was Phil's experience with Outward Bound that convinced him to found Project U.S.E. Explained Phil: "In Trenton, we worked with dropouts and potential dropouts—kids who had low self-esteem and who didn't think they could succeed at anything. You should have seen their faces when they completed their first climbs. We thought, Wow! If this program works this well in

Trenton, other New Jersey schools could use it too."

Today Project U.S.E. has been in operation for more than twenty-five years. It's still based in New Jersey, but the program also reaches out to Pennsylvania and New York. Phil's group has even taught fifth graders in an elementary school in my area.

As a former teacher in the South Bronx, I wanted to hear some inner-city success stories. "Let me tell you about Newark," said Phil. "Some people don't think Newark could produce climbers. But it does."

As Phil talked, I learned about an unusual graduation requirement at St. Benedict's Prep, a Catholic boys school in Newark made up of about seventy-five percent African American students. To graduate from ninth grade, students have to hike for seven days along the Appalachian Trail—a trekking route that runs along the Appalachian Mountains from Maine to Georgia. The trek is led by juniors and seniors trained by Project U.S.E. At the end of the trek, a teacher shakes each student's hand and says, "Congratulations! Now you're a tenth grader."

Phil also told me about a remarkable young woman named Lessonaya Ruiz. While a student at Newark's East Side High School, Lessonaya took part in one of Phil's rock-climbing trips. "She had never been more than ten blocks from her home," said Phil. "But after she came off the rocks, her face was beaming. She told me, 'I don't care what it takes, but I'm going to go to college where there are mountains.'"

To keep Lessonaya's enthusiasm alive, Project U.S.E.

granted her a scholarship to go on a climbing expedition in the Rocky Mountains of Colorado and Wyoming. Lessonaya captured her feelings in a letter home to "the gang at Project U.S.E." Wrote Lessonaya: "When I stood at the edge of a cliff and looked down, the thought of jumping terrified me. But once I jumped, I realized things are only as hard as we make them, and that there's not much we can't do if we set our minds to it. This trip has helped me to realize there is a lot more to life than what I'd seen."

Lessonaya went on to win two scholarships at Colorado State University. She also took several part-time jobs. Wrote Lessonaya in another letter, "I have a hard time explaining why I chose a college so far from home. Some of my friends just don't understand that staying close to home may be best for them, but Colorado is best for me."

Although I've never met her, I understand why Lessonaya had to travel to the mountains of Colorado. I think she'd understand, too, why I search far and wide for new mountains to climb. If you want to understand the magic that lures people like Lessonaya and me to the peaks, come join us—and climb away!